FLICKA

The Movie Novel

FOX 2000 PICTURES PRESENTS A GIL NETTER PRODUCTION "FLICKA" ALISON LOHMAN TIM McGRAW MARIA BELLO COSTUME DESIGNER MOLLY MAGINNIS MUSIC SUPERVISOR JASON ALEXANDER MUSIC BY AARON ZIGMAN CO-PRODUCER KEVIN HALLORAN FILM EDITOR ANDREW MARCUS PRODUCTION DESIGNER SHARON SEYMOUR DIRECTOR OF PHOTOGRAPHY J. MICHAEL MURO PRODUCED BY GIL NETTER BASED UPON THE NOVEL "MY FRIEND FLICKA" BY MARY O'HARA SCREENPLAY BY MARK ROSENTHAL & LAWRENCE KONNER DIRECTED BY MICHAEL MAYER

www.flickamovie.com

HarperCollins®, 📖®, and HarperKidsEntertainment™ are trademarks of HarperCollins Publishers.

Flicka: The Movie Novel
Flicka™ & © 2006 Twentieth Century Fox Film Corporation. All rights reserved.
Printed in the United States of America.
No part of this book may be used or reproduced in any manner whatsoever
without written permission except in the case of brief quotations embodied
in critical articles and reviews. For information address HarperCollins Children's Books,
a division of HarperCollins Publishers, 1350 Avenue of the Americas, New York, NY 10019.
www.harperchildrens.com

Library of Congress catalog card number: 2005933917
ISBN-10: 0-06-087606-9 — ISBN-13: 978-0-06-087606-7

Typography by Scott Richards

❖

First Edition

FLICKA

The Movie Novel

Novelization by KATHLEEN W. ZOEHFELD
Based on the Motion Picture Screenplay
by MARK ROSENTHAL & LAWRENCE KONNER
Based upon the novel "My Friend Flicka"
by MARY O'HARA

HarperKidsEntertainment
An Imprint of HarperCollinsPublishers

FLICKA

The Movie Novel

CHAPTER ONE

It was a bright June morning in Wyoming, and the students in Mr. Masterson's history class settled down at their desks to begin their final exam. Katy McLaughlin read the essay question, but she already knew what the topic would be—America's settlement of the west. And she knew what her teacher was expecting everyone to write: it had been America's destiny to expand westward, bringing its ordered homes and ranches, fences and schools—sturdy brick schools like this one, the Laramie Academy—to tame the wild and unruly land.

Katy closed her eyes for a moment and thought of her favorite painting, the one that hung above the stairwell at home on her family's ranch where she spent her summers. In the sage green and dusty hues of the prairie, it showed a herd of exuberant wild horses charging across an open range under a glittering blue sky.

She picked up her pencil. "What does it mean to follow your destiny?" she wanted to write. But certain thoughts crowded her mind—angry, rebellious thoughts; thoughts she knew Mr. Masterson would not appreciate.

Her pencil motionless, she stared out the window, daydreaming. *People say it was America's destiny to go west. Pioneers fled crowded eastern cities to find freedom and self-reliance in the wilderness. I say it was all a big con, a hoax! I wish they all stayed home,* Katy thought.

Dragging herself out of the daydream, Katy tried to rein in her ideas, tried to say something acceptable, something Mr. Masterson would think sounded studious and sensible. But her thoughts galloped away across the wide prairie, like the wild horses she imagined bursting out of their picture frame and running free.

"They called themselves settlers," her imaginary essay continued, "but there was nothing 'settled' about them. They couldn't fence the land fast enough. It happened almost overnight. The truth is, wherever a 'settler' left his footprint, there was a *hoofprint* beside it. A dog may be man's best friend, but the history of the west was written by the *horse*.

"You'd think people would've been thankful to them. But no! They couldn't rest until there was no open range left for the herds—nothing wild left in the great American wilderness. They say the American west was a paradise and it was our destiny to claim it. I say, call someplace paradise and kiss it good-bye!"

Katy was startled out of her reverie by the end-of-period bell. Most of her classmates had already finished their essays and were filing out the door. The blank pages of her exam booklet glared up at her accusingly. She twirled one of her long, dark braids until wild wispy strands began to unravel. "I've got to write something! Anything!" she thought, but there was no time.

Mr. Masterson, with his neatly trimmed beard and impeccably pressed trousers, loomed over her. "Time's up, Katy."

She stared at him, speechless, as he collected her booklet. It was a disaster! Just like the whole semester before it had been!

The next day, the Laramie Academy students, in their regulation blue blazers and green-and-blue striped school ties, gathered in the auditorium to receive their end-of-year grades. Katy rushed in late as usual. She stood apart from her classmates who were laughing and flirting and making plans to visit each other over the summer.

As the prefect entered, the students grew quiet and waited for their names to be called. "Edwards, Hansen, Bradley, Wilson, Koop . . ." the prefect called out.

Miranda Koop, a couple of years older than Katy, grabbed her report card and rushed over to Katy. "Thank God I caught you before you left," she said breathlessly. The dark-haired girl untied a bright bandana from her wrist and tied it around Katy's. "Could you give this to Howard?" she asked.

Katy's older brother, Howard, was home on the ranch helping her dad with the horses. She would be seeing him tomorrow. "Not a problem," she replied.

Katy thought about how glad she would be to see Howard again, but a knot formed in her stomach as she imagined how her father would react to her report card.

"Thanks, Katy," said Miranda. "I think I'll be seeing a lot of you this summer."

Miranda's friend Gracie sailed past them. "See you next year!" she cried.

"See you in September, Gracie!" sang Miranda cheerfully.

As Miranda breezed away with her friends, Katy found herself face-to-face with the prefect.

"McLaughlin," he said, holding out an official white envelope emblazoned with the academy crest. "You need to see the headmaster."

Katy took the envelope. She did not even have to open it

to know what the headmaster was going to say. After this year's troubles, there was no way she would be promoted to the next grade.

She climbed aboard the school van and crawled into the backseat, hoping no one would notice her. It felt good to be on the road, watching the flat, ugly sprawl of the city receding behind her. Soon she was looking out the window at the beautiful green short-grass hills of Wyoming.

Near dusk, they pulled up at a service station. Six kids tumbled out and rushed into their parents' waiting arms. Katy could see the Neversummer Mountains in the distance. Her family home was a couple of hours farther on—a majestic horse ranch high in the foothills. She imagined her father meeting her in their maroon Chevy truck. She clutched the official white envelope, damp and crumpled in her fist like an empty tube of toothpaste.

The sun had set and the crickets were singing by the time Katy spotted her dad's tall, slim silhouette leaning against the side of the truck. The van pulled up beside him. Katy hesitated, staying rooted to her seat so long that her dad had to crane his neck and peer in to see if she was there. She slid out of the van, and the driver honked a friendly farewell.

Rob McLaughlin lifted Katy's suitcases as if they were feathers and tossed them into the flatbed. Then he gave his daughter a big bear hug. "Seems like I dropped you off yesterday," he cried.

"Daddy . . ." she said, snuggling against his broad chest.

Rob grabbed a cowboy hat from the cab and popped it on Katy's head. "Let's go home," he said.

Home at the ranch, Katy's mother, Nell, busied herself in the kitchen with a lump of bread dough. She squeezed it with her long slender fingers, pressed it with the heels of her hands, and pounded it with her fists.

Dinner sat waiting in covered dishes. She and Howard had already hung a "Welcome Home, Katy!" banner over the door and put up some festive decorations in honor of the big day. Howard sat reading a book. He glanced up, amused at seeing his mother trying so desperately to keep busy.

"Mom . . ." he said.

"I know, I know . . . chill," replied Nell.

"You got it."

Then all of a sudden, the dogs were barking, and Howard and Nell could hear a familiar horn tooting merrily in the distance.

Howard leaped up so fast he nearly knocked over his chair. They both raced to the front porch and stared at the headlights coming down the long, steep road.

When the pickup came to a stop, Nell bounded off the porch and pulled open the cab door. Rob put a finger to his lips. Katy was fast asleep. Nell touched Rob's arm gently, savoring the moment. She looked at Katy lovingly, feeling the weeks, the months, they had spent apart. She shook Katy's shoulder gently. Katy opened her eyes and instinctually scrambled out of the truck.

Nell glanced past her into the cab. "Anyone seen my daughter?" she teased.

Katy rubbed her eyes, momentarily confused.

Nell pretended to inspect Katy as if she'd never seen her

before. "Do I know you?"

"Mom . . ." cried Katy. She smiled broadly and wrapped her mother in her arms.

"Oh, I've missed you," said Nell.

Katy ran to Howard and gave him a big hug, too. As their parents headed inside to get dinner on the table, brother and sister hung back. She untied the bandana from around her wrist and tied it around Howard's. "This is from your fan club," she joked.

Howard smiled. But he could tell something was troubling her. "You okay?" he asked.

"He's gonna kill me," she whispered.

"How bad could it be?" he asked.

"Worse."

Rob appeared at the kitchen door, holding it open for the kids.

"You can tell me later," whispered Howard.

"I think your mother will finally sleep straight through tonight," said Rob, content at the thought of his family being reunited again for the whole summer.

CHAPTER TWO

The next morning, Katy woke up before dawn. She put on a shirt and jeans and socks, grabbed her cowboy boots, and tiptoed down the stairs. She stopped for a moment to stare at her favorite painting—the wild horses running free. She sighed happily. That's what it felt like to be home on Goose Creek Ranch—wild and free.

The screen door banged shut behind her as she slipped out through the kitchen door. She cringed. Had anyone heard? Everything in the house remained still. Katy pulled on her boots and ran as fast as she could, past the pile of rails and the big bundle of wire that would be used for new fencing, past her mom's vegetable garden, past the low-slung henhouse, and straight into the big white horse barn.

Twenty heads turned and peered at her from their stalls. The horses whinnied, and Katy's face lit up with delight. "Who feels like running?" she cried. She slipped a bridle on Yankee, a tall chestnut gelding, and before the first rooster crowed, she had ridden out through the pasture gate and was galloping bareback across the valley. It had been a rainy spring, and the high meadows were ablaze with wildflowers. Katy and Yankee plunged down the steep bank toward Goose Creek. They splashed through the water, with Katy ducking under the low-hanging branches of the cottonwood trees. They struggled up the far bank and then ran along the gentle slope, into the woods on the other side.

Katy and Yankee didn't stop until they reached the domed summit overlooking the whole valley—Katy's favorite thinking spot. There they paused and watched the rays of morning sun touching their world with gold. Katy pulled the crumpled envelope from her pocket and her eyes filled with tears. "What am I going to do?" she wondered.

Suddenly Yankee snorted and balked. He bucked once, and Katy drew in the reins. "Stop it . . . c'mon . . ." she coaxed. But something had startled the young gelding. Before she knew it, he was tearing down the steep rocky side of the hill, bucking and whinnying.

"Settle down," Katy tried to soothe him. "You want to go home, huh? Well, I guess I can't hide from him forever."

Then she heard the low guttural rumble that Yankee's sharp ears had picked up before hers. It made the hairs on her neck stand on end. She drew a deep breath. No mistaking it— that was the growl of a mountain lion!

"Quiet now," she whispered to Yankee. She thought she saw a shadow moving through the brush. Yankee reared up and pawed the air, and Katy went flying backward. She landed on her rear, but still clutched the reins tight like her father had taught her.

"Whoa! Hold on now," she cried. She grabbed a handful

of Yankee's mane and tried to jump back on. "Shhh . . . good boy," she cajoled.

But Yankee snapped his head up in wild terror. The reins jerked out of her hands, and in an instant the horse had fled. Katy stood motionless. The big cat was circling her! She could see its yellow eyes glinting in the shadows. She took a step toward the thornbushes and saw them shimmy. The lion was there, ready to spring!

Katy's father had taught her the hard-and-fast rule— when confronted with a big cat, face your enemy and try to look as tough and scary as you can. Never, never try to outrun one. But Katy bolted and ran. She careened down the hillside, branches and thorns catching in her long hair and tearing at her clothes and skin.

"Owwwww!" she cried as she tripped over a stone at the bottom of the hill. She landed flat on her face in the middle of a meadow abloom with deep blue delphinium. Just a short distance away, a wild horse heard the cry, lifted her head from the dense grass, and peered in Katy's direction.

Katy raised her gaze and looked up at the beautiful, ebony filly. The young filly's mane was caked with mud and twisted up with burrs and nettles, just like Katy's hair.

The horse cried out and reared up on her hind feet, windmilling her forehooves in the air over Katy's head.

"Don't hurt me," she cried. She rolled out of the way and covered her head with her arms. The wild horse rushed past her. When Katy looked up again, she saw that the horse was not charging *her,* she was trying to scare away the mountain lion!

The big cat growled. The horse screamed and reared again, pawing the air fiercely. Finally the lion gave up and slunk away through the grass.

"You scared him off," whispered Katy.

But the horse wasn't ready to calm down. She charged toward Katy, who ducked and rolled once again. The horse snorted angrily and galloped away. Katy stood on tiptoe and watched the wild mustang disappear into the distance on her long elegant legs. Then Katy turned and raced back home as fast as she could, hoping to find Yankee along the way.

CHAPTER THREE

Before breakfast that morning, rodeo entrepreneur Norbert Rye arrived at the ranch pulling his long, shiny horse trailer. He was there to pick up the quarter horses he had purchased from the McLaughlins the other day. Jack and Gus, Rob's steady ranch hands, led the horses into the trailer, one by one.

Norbert stood to the side, talking with Nell. "Rob's kinda quiet this morning," he observed.

"Oh, he gets that way when he's busy," replied Nell.

Norbert was not convinced. "Your husband is what I call an opinionated man."

"His opinion is . . ." Nell hesitated, "last year you bought twice as many head from us."

"Last year is twelve months obsolete, ain't it," quipped Norbert.

At that moment, Rob rode up on his favorite gelding and swung himself down from the saddle. "Norbert, this is your lucky day," he cried.

"That right?" asked Norbert skeptically.

"Ready to meet a miracle on four legs?" asked Rob. "I've been saving him just for you. Three-year-old stallion. Isn't he something, honey?" He turned to Nell for confirmation.

"A beauty," she agreed.

"Don't need any more quarter horses," said Norbert. "Any profit for the middle man in the horse business is fading faster than a mountain sunset."

"Howard will bring him 'round," said Rob.

"Don't need 'em at the rodeo, either," Norbert continued. "Folks are bored with barrel races and calf roping."

"Howard!" called Rob.

Norbert was getting impatient. "Here's my check. So long."

Rob didn't take it. He held up his hand and asked Norbert to wait.

Howard finally stumbled out of the house buttoning up his shirt. He was headed for the barn.

"I do not need any more horses," said Norbert turning back toward his truck.

He paused for a moment. "Unless you have something a little more *interesting*."

"For instance?" asked Rob.

"*Mistengos,*" said Norbert.

Nell grimaced. She knew Norbert had just pushed Rob's biggest button.

"Mustangs?" cried Rob.

"That's right," said Norbert. "Wild horses. The more loco the better."

"Morning," Howard greeted them, trying to look wide awake.

"No mustangs around here," said Rob, ignoring Howard. "Those four-legged parasites can strip ten acres of grassland overnight. Starve a man's herd."

Nell and Howard stood by powerless, knowing the heated cowboy talk that would ensue.

"Wild horse racing's my biggest draw," insisted Norbert. "Had a purse last year near ten thousand dollars."

"Only takes one mustang foal to ruin a herd," argued Rob. "Then my quarter horses wouldn't be pure quarter horse anymore, would they?"

"If you had a herd of mustangs around, I'd buy them all," declared Norbert.

"If I had a herd of mustangs around, I'd be ruined," Rob insisted.

"Yep, I sure miss seeing horses run wild," mused Norbert.

"Now I'll tell you what you don't see," cried Rob.

Nell and Howard knew the lecture that was coming. They'd heard it all a dozen times before.

"You don't see 'em crippled when their hooves splinter.

Or starvin' when their teeth grow too long to chew. You don't see worms in their bellies or the nettles in their manes. Drives 'em loco . . . and once they're loco, they're as good as dead." Rob shook his head in disagreement with Norbert. "My horses thank God every night I own 'em. They blow kisses when I walk into the barn."

Norbert sighed and handed Nell the check. "Always a delight to see you, Nell. As for your husband . . . gelding would be my suggestion." He strode to his truck and drove off down the long prairie road.

Nell and Rob looked at each other, worried.

"There goes the money we've already spent," said Rob.

"No rancher wins a reputation for how he handles *good* luck," said Nell encouragingly. "We'll get by, like always."

But Rob turned his anxiety on Howard. "Well? Call your sister," he ordered. "Start mucking the stalls."

"Yes, sir," said Howard.

As Rob stormed off, Howard whispered to Nell, "She took off before I got up."

Nell digested this for a moment. "I should call your father

back," she said halfheartedly. "Oh, Rob," she whispered, making a small waving motion with her hand.

Howard laughed. "I'll do the stalls myself," he said, feeling a kinship with his mother's bright and easygoing manner.

Nell gave him a kiss on the cheek, and hurried back to her desk in the kitchen, where she input Norbert Rye's sale in the ranch ledger. She stirred pancake batter absentmindedly as she stared at the year's finances on the computer screen. Rob was right. Things didn't look good.

She decided to shut down the computer, when the annoying beep of the fax machine interrupted her. The fax did not offer any good news, either. She handed it to Rob as he entered, giving him a worried glance. He looked it over, folded it up, and put it in his pocket.

Nell slid a stack of golden pancakes onto a big platter.

Gus and Jack dusted themselves off after their morning chores and entered for breakfast.

"Where's Katy?" asked Rob.

"I think she must've taken Yankee out," replied Gus. Gus was older than Jack, in his late thirties, and simply adored Katy.

Nell set the platter on the table. "And for your dining pleasure, wild gooseberry pancakes and rosemary chicken sausages."

"Who lives better than us?" exclaimed Rob.

"Let me think . . . the Windsors?" said Howard, sliding into his chair.

"Speaking of which, you gonna put your brand on that little school girl this summer?" Jack asked him. "When she walks, she's got that . . . *hmmm-mmm-mmm.*"

"Oh, we stopped branding our females a few years ago. Isn't that right, Rob?" joked Nell.

Rob smiled. "I kind of miss it, though."

Nell poked him in the ribs.

Jack, his dark handsome eyes twinkling playfully, pointed his fork at Howard. "Take it from an expert. Don't let that little flicka get away."

"The little what?" asked Nell.

"Means 'pretty girl' or somethin,'" explained Jack. "That's what Gus calls Katy."

"He does?" asked Nell.

"A flicka is just a young girl, innocent. You can see in her face the beauty she will become," said Gus in his soft, earnest voice. "I think it's Swedish. My mama used to call my little sister 'flicka.'"

"Outstanding recovery," cried Howard.

At that, Katy tumbled through the door, breathless, scratched up, and dirty. Her hair was a tangled mess of burrs and mud.

"A lion! On the mountain! Dad . . . right there in front of me . . ." Katy tried to tell her story so fast the words came out in a jumble.

"You're bleeding," said Nell, rushing to her side.

"I saw it," cried Katy. "And a horse . . . a mustang . . . Dad . . . it ran off the lion!"

"Slow down," said Rob. "Which was it, a lion or a horse?"

Nell began dabbing the scratches on Katy's face with a wet washcloth.

"Both!" cried Katy. "Aren't you going to do something!?"

"Where'd you see this lion?" asked Rob.

"I'm not sure. It just all happened so fast. But it was there."

"Did you see Sasquatch, too?" teased Jack.

"Did someone ask your opinion?" snapped Katy.

But Nell was truly upset. "Would a lion come that close?" she asked. "In daylight? I mean, would it attack the ranch?"

"Lions will attack anything, any place, any time," replied Rob.

"You're supposed to say, 'They're as afraid of us as we are of them,'" said Nell.

Rob turned and looked her in the eye. "They're as afraid of us as we are of them," he parroted.

"It was a lion. *Honest!*" insisted Katy.

"As long as we're being honest," said Rob, "is there something you need to tell me?"

Katy froze.

"About school?" Rob prompted.

He dug into his pocket and pulled out the fax. He unfolded it and handed it to Katy.

Nell and Howard were dying for her.

"Not one word? And two hours for the exam!?" he demanded.

"I wrote it in my head," explained Katy. "I just didn't get a chance . . . to put it down."

"In your head. Uh-huh."

Nell cringed, knowing that in Rob's mind Katy had said about the worst thing possible.

"Wouldn't have made a difference anyway," said Katy defiantly. "They just want us to spit back exactly what they want to hear. I *have* an opinion. It's just not *their* opinion."

"Their opinion is that you should repeat the year," cried Rob. "Throw it away. Money down the drain!"

Katy was in trouble. She could see her father was really agitated now. He stood up from the breakfast table and paced.

"Do you realize what this family goes without just to pay for your private education?" he fumed. "Truck passing two hundred thousand miles? Let's see if it'll go another fifty. Generator shot? Oh, we'll just keep fixing it. Barn roof ready to blow away? Patch it. *Again.* For the umpteenth time. Your mom's never had a warm-weather vacation.... " Rob ranted on, blaming Katy for all his failures.

"I don't need it," Nell interjected, helplessly.

"Yes, you do," cried Rob. "All this so you can go to a fancy boarding school." He threw out his arms in utter amazement. "But I go along, 'cause your mother wants you to go to college...."

"Your father wants it, too," added Nell.

"Now we have to worry if she'll even *graduate.*"

"Katy, you can go to your brother's school—the University of Manual Labor," said Jack, desperate to lighten the mood.

Whereas she could never have contradicted her father, twenty-four-year-old Jack was fair game. Katy rocketed out of her chair and tried to give him a good pummeling. Jack had his hands full holding her off.

"Just teasing!" he cried.

"Enough," declared Rob.

They stopped immediately.

"Since everyone's so full of energy . . . we've got fence line to repair, a mound of manure to spread . . . lots of fun stuff."

Jack and Gus rose and headed for the door. Jack thought again and came back to grab two more pancakes for the road.

"Didn't I already feed you?" joked Nell.

"Was that today?" asked Jack innocently.

As Rob left with the men, Katy stayed in the kitchen with her mother, not saying a thing.

But nothing could hold Katy behind for long. Howard, Gus, and Jack were loading the three-ton truck with fence posts, while Rob kept careful count.

"Sixteen, eighteen, twenty . . . Not those, Howard. Can't you see the rot?" complained Rob.

Katy ran up behind her father. "Dad!" she cried. "I think we should bring that mustang in."

"Not now, Katy," said Rob. "That's twenty, twenty-two, twenty-four . . ."

"That lion can take down a horse," she argued.

Rob spun around and glared at her. "Katy!"

"I could probably find her again," said Katy.

Rob jumped down from the flatbed and spoke to her eye-to-eye. "No!" he declared.

"I'll help her," offered Howard.

Rob stared at Howard, shocked that his son would contradict him. "This doesn't concern you, does it?"

Katy could see her brother chafing at their father's temper.

Rob turned back to Katy. "If you live on a ranch, you have to *contribute*. That's how we get by. Do your chores, help your mother. Otherwise, I want you to write that essay. Maybe I can talk them into passing you."

"Yes, sir," said Katy.

Rob adjusted his hat, his voice softening. "Then we'll talk about horses."

CHAPTER FOUR

Back at the house, Katy slumped in a metal folding chair, clutching a big wet bullfrog. She cuddled the stout amphibian in her arms as if it were a little baby. Nell had placed the chair under the one big shade tree in the yard. She brought out her scissors, wanting to trim Katy's unruly hair.

"Just a few inches for the summer," Nell said.

"No," said Katy crossly.

Nell held the scissors motionless in the air. "I get better-reasoned arguments from the hens," she quipped.

"Short hair makes me look like a boy," Katy cried.

"That would be impossible," Nell reassured her. "You're a flicka."

Katy looked up at her questioningly.

"A pretty girl," Nell explained. "You can ask Gus."

Nell's scissors began snipping. "How's your friend, Stephanie?" she asked.

"Shallow, vain, insincere . . . the usual."

Nell was surprised. "Since when?"

"Since Eric. Or was it Justin?" said Katy. "Lost track. And then when he dumps her, she's my 'best friend' again."

Nell sensed that Katy was sad in a way she hadn't seen before. "You never know what'll happen," she encouraged her. "People can surprise you."

"I guess so." Katy shrugged.

Finishing up the haircut, Nell dumped a bucket of water on Katy's head.

"Ahhhh! Cold!" she cried, laughing.

Then it was time to go back upstairs and work on her essay.

Katy sat at her desk for a long time, tilting back in her chair and daydreaming. She imagined the wild black mustang running through a mountain forest.

In time, almost everything wild had vanished from the west, she wrote in her mind. *Or so the people believed. A few wild horses,* mistengos, *hid away in the mountains. But people hunted them and sold them to slaughterhouses. Some said they ruined the land for cattle. Isolated and hungry, they were on their way to disappearing from the face of the earth. . . .*

Suddenly Katy remembered those yellow eyes flashing in the bushes. She rocked the front legs of her chair back to the floor with a bang. She sprang up and abandoned her test booklet, still blank. A breeze blew through her open window, the lace curtains framing the beautiful mountains in the distance. That, she decided, was where she belonged, not here chained to a desk.

Nell was pulling out a tangle of weeds in the garden when she spotted Katy sneaking out toward the stables. She dreaded to think what would happen if Rob found out. But Katy was so close to her own heart, Nell understood what was calling her to go.

She smiled and whispered, "Get back here, Katy," as she watched her daughter galloping off down the valley.

This time Katy had actually saddled Yankee, and she brought along a rope as well. She rode up to her favorite lookout again and scanned the horizon for the mustang. She simply had to find her before that mountain lion returned.

She and Yankee moved slowly down the slope. Yankee stepped high over a fallen tree and then came to an abrupt halt. The wild horse was standing right before them, her face deep in the grass. When she saw Yankee's fright, the filly whinnied.

Before Katy could do a thing, the mustang kicked backward and fled across the meadow.

Katy urged Yankee to follow, but he put his head down and bucked.

"No way can you buck me from a saddle," cried Katy. "Now, move out!"

She kept her eyes glued to the wild horse as it zigzagged through the woods. Hard as the filly tried, she could not shake Katy and Yankee. Katy sat forward in her saddle, edging closer and closer. She lifted the rope off the saddle horn.

Katy could feel exactly what the young filly was feeling at this moment—if she could only ride fast enough, long enough, she could outrun all the fearful things in this world. They could never catch her. Katy let out a wild scream.

The filly reared up on her hind legs. Katy stood in her stirrups and threw her lariat. The loop slipped over the filly's head. She had her! But the wild horse's strength proved too much for Katy. The filly spun, launching herself in the air with incredible force. Katy felt herself being yanked from the saddle. She landed with a thud, dug her heels in the ground, and tried to slow the filly down. But it was a tug-of-war she could not win. The mustang ran hard, pulling Katy along, running and stumbling, behind.

Rob and Howard and the men were just one ridge over, rounding up the main herd of quarter horses. Howard rode up next to his dad, looking for an opportunity to tell him something that had been troubling him for a long time. But before he had a chance to say anything, Rob turned to him.

"How do they look?" he asked.

"Well . . ." Howard hesitated. "Pretty much the same as yesterday." He knew his father wanted him to feel the same enthusiasm for the horses that he did, but he just didn't feel it.

"They can change in a heartbeat," said Rob.

"Right," said Howard. He wondered how he was ever going to find the courage to tell his dad how he really felt.

"Animals are like us, son," Rob continued. "They'll always find a way to tell you exactly what they're feeling. You just have to learn to listen to them. Let's bring 'em in!"

Howard and Rob and Jack and Gus worked the herd from opposite ends. Rob paused for a moment, sensing something was amiss.

"Something's bothering them!" he shouted to Jack.

Jack stopped and listened. "I don't hear anything."

"Shhh," Rob said to the horses in a soothing tone, "just relax and let me do the worrying."

The men rode back and forth trying to control the herd,

but the horses were becoming increasingly alert and skittish.

"Let's try to keep 'em moving," Rob called to the men.

At that moment, the source of their anxiety appeared on the crest of the hill above. The wild black mustang came thundering down the slope, with Katy—battered and covered in dust—rolling down behind her.

The filly set her wild eyes on Rob and let out a terrible scream. Rob shouted at her and beat his rope against his leg, ready to swing his lariat at the first opportunity. But the filly ran free, taking half the herd along with her.

Rob's horse bucked in protest, and he tried in vain to settle him down.

Jack looked at the chaos in the herd. "Don't even *think* about getting in the middle of that!" he cried.

"Let them run it out, Dad," said Howard sensibly.

"Right," said Rob, meaning "fat chance!" He urged his horse into a gallop and tore off after the herd.

As he watched his dad reacting in the heat of anger, Howard felt in his gut the uselessness of gestures like his father's. This, he thought, was exactly why he was so frustrated with the whole ranching business.

"What's wrong with him?" he asked, helplessly.

"If it was somebody else, I'd be worried," said Jack. "But that's your father."

With sheer force and determination, Rob roped the wild filly and pulled her away from the herd. Jack and Gus hurried in and hurled two more ropes over her head. The filly's eyes blazed with rage as she tried one last time to rear up and break free of the constricting ropes. Foam dripped from her mouth and sweat poured from her sides.

As her father strode to where she was standing, Katy watched his shadow approaching on the ground. She glanced up, but the look in her father's eyes was almost as frightening as the look in the wild filly's.

Katy kicked the ground with her toe. "I didn't want the lion to get my horse."

"*Your* horse!?" cried Rob. "That mangy beast doesn't belong to you or anyone. Must've separated from some wild herd. I'm surprised it's still alive."

"What are you gonna do with her?" Katy asked.

"Don't want to do a thing with this loco creature," declared Rob. "Ain't worth the price of a bale of hay."

"Isn't Norbert looking for broncos?" Gus quietly reminded him.

Rob considered this for a moment. "Let's get it behind a fence . . . but keep it clear of the herd."

Gus and Jack pulled the filly, screaming at the end of their ropes.

Howard picked up Yankee's reins and led him over to Katy. "Nice of you to drop in," he said.

"Did you see her stride?" Katy asked. "Isn't she amazing?"

Howard couldn't help thinking how similar Katy and their father really were. But before he could answer, he heard his father shouting for him to come and help.

CHAPTER FIVE

From the front porch, Nell could see the men and Katy approaching with the herd. Her face lit up in anticipation. Howard cantered up ahead of the others and dismounted.

She could read him like a book. Something was wrong. "How bad?" she asked. "Give me a category."

Howard glanced back at his father. "Oh, I don't think he's made a category for this one yet."

Nell saw Rob trying to wrangle in the wild mustang.

"Open the pen!" he shouted.

Gus swung the gate open. The filly reared up, fighting

Rob and Jack every step of the way.

"She's scared to go through," said Gus.

Katy tied Yankee up and ran to greet her mom. "Come look at her!" she cried.

Nell blanched. "*This* is the horse she was talking about?" she asked Howard.

Howard nodded.

Finally the men forced the filly into the round holding pen. Katy climbed up and perched atop the white plank fence. Rob slipped the ropes off the filly's neck and rode out as Jack swung the gate shut.

The filly threw a fit so terrible it was frightening to watch.

"This is a dangerous animal," declared Rob.

"She's just scared," said Katy.

"I'd say she's about two years old," observed Nell.

"That means two years wild," said Rob. "And I'd bet most of it was spent alone."

Still the filly cried loudly, racing in a tight circle around the pen.

"She'll calm down once I start training her," Katy declared.

But her father had a different plan. "This horse will never be ridden," he snapped. "I'm calling Norbert after dinner."

"No," whined Katy, "I can ride her."

"No, you can't," cried Rob. "The wildness is in her blood. A horse like this has been fighting every day of its life. It's crazy enough to kill somebody."

Katy would've kept the argument going all day, but Rob held up his hands and stopped it once and for all. "Nobody goes in there without my permission," he declared and stormed off.

Katy's insides hurt as she watched the filly's wild rage. "Calm down, Flicka," she coaxed.

"You named her?" asked Nell.

"*Flicka*," said Katy. She looked up at Gus. "That's the word, isn't it?"

"Yes, um, beautiful young girl," said Gus shyly.

"Well," chuckled Jack, "you got the *girl* part right."

Dinner that night was an unnaturally quiet affair. Rob tried his best to ignore Katy's presence, and Katy kept her eyes focused on her plate. The longer the silence went on, the more strain everyone felt.

"I didn't see the vet bill," Rob said at last.

"Somebody grab this last burger," said Nell, hoping to deflect his attention from yet another loaded subject.

Rob looked at her. "How much?" he demanded.

"Know what I've been thinking about?" she said lightly. "If quitters never win, why are you supposed to quit while you are ahead?"

Howard loved his mother's sense of humor. "Or how good can a bedtime story be if it's supposed to put you to sleep?" he added.

"*How much?*" insisted Rob.

"Oh, I can't remember exactly. . . ." Nell hedged. "Well, sixteen hundred dollars."

"Sixteen hundred," Rob cried. "That's just unacceptable."

"I'll speak to the horses about it," Nell joked.

"I don't remember my daddy giving horses shots. Horses

used to be healthy," Rob said gruffly. "Took care of themselves. Ain't that right, Gus?"

"Oh, sure," said Gus. "Back then, the horses mucked their own stalls, nailed on their own shoes, even chipped in with the rent money."

Jack laughed.

"Don't call Norbert," pleaded Katy.

Everyone fell silent again and stared at her.

Nell signaled Rob not to say anything.

He composed himself, looked away from Katy, and asked Nell to please pass him that hamburger.

Katy went up to her room and stared out her window at the horses milling in the paddock like shadows dancing in the moonlight.

"I don't care what he says. She's my horse," she declared as her mom joined her at the window.

"Calm down. Give me a chance to talk to him," said Nell.

Katy slipped into bed. "But he doesn't listen when he's this mad."

Nell sat down beside her. "Oh, you know what they say. Anger's just fear on the way out."

"Nice try," said Katy. "He's not afraid of anything."

"I don't know." Nell chuckled. "You could scare the heck out of anybody."

"Yeah, right," said Katy skeptically.

"When you were three, you climbed out of bed, unlatched the kitchen door, and walked out. Your father found you at the slough in the bull pasture. Either one could've killed you. You were laughing all the way home."

"I don't remember that at all," Katy sighed.

Nell smiled. "He does. Parents get a kind of selective memory. Sometimes I'm so busy I can't remember yesterday. But I swear I can catalog every injury, every close call, every 'another-inch-and-they-could've-been-killed' that has ever happened to my children."

Katy reached out and grabbed her mother's warm hand.

"Try to understand what it's like to feel responsible for something you love so much," said Nell. She kissed Katy, tucked her in, and turned off the lights.

When Nell entered her own bedroom, Rob was already in bed. She slipped in beside him.

"Give her the horse," she said.

He turned and looked at her. "No."

"Training her own horse will set a pattern to her days," argued Nell. "She needs to feel good about something . . . about *herself*."

"Here it comes . . . the psychological gobbledygook." Rob rolled his eyes disdainfully. "This isn't about psychology. It's about discipline. I am not going to reward bad behavior."

Nell prodded him in the ribs. "That sure sounds like psychology to me."

He sat straight up. *"No horse!"* Slowly he settled back down, leaning against the headboard. He stewed in worried silence.

"The township called again," said Nell. "They're desperate for someone with a college degree. And I already know their computer program."

"It's a two-hour drive each way," grumbled Rob.

"I don't mind."

"We'll never see each other," said Rob. "End up leaving notes on the door as we pass by."

"Sounds kind of romantic," said Nell. "And a dependable paycheck would take some of the pressure off."

"We'll get by," said Rob.

"And I wouldn't mind getting out a bit, seeing other people once in a while," added Nell.

"You're right. I can't be 'other people!'" Rob began to shout in frustration. "I can't make this life easier. This is the way it will always be. Either we hold on 'til things get better, or . . . I don't care . . . I'll sell the place!"

"Lower your voice," whispered Nell.

They glanced behind them at the wall that divided their room from Katy's.

"When I had Katy's room, I could hear my parents talking. But I couldn't hear what they were saying," said Rob. "I thought they were telling bedtime stories to each other. Really cool, secret stories. I thought, 'One day they'll tell me those stories, too.'"

Nell felt his hurt and shared his sadness.

"Now I realize they were probably just arguing over bills," said Rob. "Trying to figure out ways they could save a little more money. There was no time for 'cool stories.'"

Nell snuggled close beside him. "I know a cool story."

He smiled and sighed and gathered her into his arms.

CHAPTER SIX

While the grown-ups were drifting off to sleep, Katy crept out of bed and tiptoed out to the paddock. She climbed the white board fence and watched Flicka in silence for a long time. The filly paced and whinnied relentlessly, searching for any possibility of escape.

Katy began to hum a quiet soothing song. Flicka paused for just a moment. Thinking she finally had the horse's attention, Katy jumped into the paddock. "Hey, girl," she whispered.

But Flicka turned on her and charged. Startled, Katy dove under the fence rail. She stood up and dusted herself off.

"Sorry, girl. That was my fault." She went to the barn, grabbed a few apples from a bucket, and stuffed them in her back pocket. Thus armed with treats and still singing, she tried climbing back into the paddock. Flicka ignored her. Katy took a step closer. Flicka looked up. Katy stood as still as she could.

The horse whinnied and kicked and began to trot nervously around the paddock again. Katy slowly pulled one of the apples from her pocket and offered it in her outstretched palm.

The filly stared at her, interested.

"You want it?" coaxed Katy. "Come and get it. But you'd have to trust me to do that, wouldn't you?"

Flicka stepped gingerly, just close enough to stretch out her long neck and reach the apple with her lips.

Moving ever so slowly, Katy reached up and ran her hand across Flicka's neck and mane. "You know me," she said softly. She took another apple from her pocket, and Flicka reached out again and greedily snapped it in two with her teeth.

Katy smiled from the inside, hoping not to jinx this perfect moment. "I'm not so bad, right?" She ran her hand along Flicka's flank, singing softly the whole time.

"Good girl," she whispered.

It was high time she got herself back to bed, but Katy could not take her eyes off the filly. She kneeled by the fence and rested her head on the bottom rail.

The next thing she knew, Jack was shaking her shoulder gently. She opened her eyes to the early dawn light. "What . . . ?" she asked, confused.

"Maybe you should wash up," said Jack quietly. "Someone might think you slept here all night."

He helped her to her feet. She rubbed the kinks out of her stiff legs and hurried back to the house. On her way, she glanced over her shoulder and gave Jack a grateful smile. If her father had caught her there, she could only imagine what his fury would be like. Jack had saved her in more ways than one.

* * *

That afternoon, Rob told Howard and Katy to drive the truck out on the range and fix the fence. Katy held each post steady while Howard took out the pliers and twisted the wire taut. He could see she was fading from exhaustion. He wiped the sweat from his brow and trimmed the ends of the wire.

"You can have Chariot," he said, referring to his favorite gelding.

"It's not the same thing," said Katy.

"Four legs. A tail. Food goes in the front, comes out the back," said Howard.

"As long as you're here, he'll be yours."

"No problem. . . . 'Cause I won't be here," declared Howard.

Katy stared at him. "I mean . . . on the ranch."

"I know what you mean," said Howard. "I said I'd give the ranch a try. I tried it. It's not working for me. I think I'm going to take that scholarship from B.U. . . . If I can borrow somebody's backbone." Howard smiled at Katy. "So will you tell him for me?"

Katy couldn't believe what she was hearing. "Why would you want to leave Wyoming?"

Howard scratched his head and pretended to ponder the question deeply. "Oh, I don't know, how about restaurants where you don't have to drive up to the window . . . or—"

"But he needs you to keep the ranch going," Katy interrupted.

"Keep your voice down," said Howard in mock seriousness.

But Katy was surprised. She looked around for someone who might be listening. "Nobody can hear us way out here."

"Oh, this whole place is bugged," joked Howard. "He's got hidden cameras and microphones everywhere."

Finally Katy was laughing, too.

Howard held a fence post up to his mouth like a microphone. "Can you read me, Dad? Over."

Then, in all seriousness he said, "He doesn't need me, Katy. You're the one he needs. He just doesn't see it yet."

CHAPTER SEVEN

The next night, Katy once again slipped out to the paddock after everyone had gone to bed. Singing her soothing song, she held up a saddle blanket and tried running it lightly over Flicka's back.

"Okay, that's so nice and soft, I'm just gonna leave it there," said Katy sweetly.

Flicka fidgeted a little, but she finally seemed to accept the blanket. Katy lifted the rope halter off the fence post and eased it closer. This was going to be a bigger challenge. Katy took a deep breath and slowly slipped the halter over Flicka's head.

The filly reared up and caught Katy in the shoulder with one of her hooves. Katy fell to the ground and rolled under the fence to safety. She clutched her bruised shoulder, groaning as she watched Flicka tear around the paddock, screaming and shaking her head until she'd shimmied herself free of the halter.

After a few more nights of patient effort and soft singing, Katy had finally convinced Flicka to accept the halter. She held the lead line and walked the filly around the paddock. Katy was itching to find out if Flicka would let her mount.

"You as bored as me?" she asked. Katy ran her hand along the horse's back. "I've got to find out sometime. . . . might as well be now."

She took a deep breath, grabbed a fistful of Flicka's mane, and vaulted on. She gritted her teeth, ready for anything. But Flicka remained perfectly still. Katy finally exhaled. But the second she relaxed, the filly took advantage of the moment to lower her head and buck violently. Katy went flying head over heels. She bounced hard on the ground. She shook off the pain and limped out of the paddock as quickly as she could. The sun was just rising over the mountaintops. Another night was ending, and just minimal progress had been made. Katy turned to Flicka with tears of frustration in her eyes.

As the week wore on, Nell was getting worried about Katy's constant fatigue. One day, she went into Katy's room a little past noon. Katy was sprawled on her bed, sleeping. "Want to take a ride to the store?" Nell asked, touching Katy gently. She spotted Katy's essay booklet on her desk and flipped through it. Nothing. Katy had not even begun, and here she was, so sound asleep that Nell didn't have the heart to wake her. She drew the curtains closed and tiptoed out.

The next night, Katy stole out to see Flicka, more determined than ever. She stuffed her shirt and jeans with rags and put on her quilted jean jacket. All padded up like a football linebacker, she stood by the fence holding Flicka's halter and blanket. "Hey, girl," she said softly.

Flicka stopped and looked at her, then turned away, uninterested.

"He said you would never carry anyone on your back," mused Katy. "How can he be right?"

She inched closer to the horse. "Good girl. . . ."

Suddenly Flicka turned and charged toward her in a rage. Katy froze in her tracks, terrified.

Jack was just getting home from an evening off. He got out of his truck and was crossing in front of the paddock when he sensed something was amiss in the familiar surroundings. He peered into the ring and saw Flicka—enraged and charging toward a paralyzed Katy. Jolted into action, Jack dove into the paddock and lunged at Katy. His momentum sent both of them tumbling toward the side of the pen. Together they wiggled under the rails. They stared back in amazement as the wild mustang threw the worst fit they'd seen yet. Katy wondered if maybe her father was right. Maybe Flicka *was* loco.

"You're not supposed to go in there," said Jack.

"What's it to you?" snapped Katy.

"You could get hurt," he replied. "Besides, that's what your father said."

"How long are you gonna be afraid of my father?" she taunted.

"Um, forever. How 'bout you?" Jack smiled.

Katy felt sorry for snapping at him. "I can ride her," she bragged.

"If you're so sure, why are you sneaking out here in the middle of the night?" he asked gently.

"Because I *have* to," declared Katy. She looked into his eyes, hoping he would understand.

Jack took her determined expression to heart. "Then don't let nobody stop you," he declared.

Disarmed by his reply, Katy stammered her thanks as he turned to walk back to the barn.

CHAPTER EIGHT

The morning dawned, warm and cloudless, and Nell got to work in the barn with Jack, brushing two black quarter horses till their coats shined, ready for their delivery to the Koop ranch.

"They're buying them, not marrying them," quipped Rob.

Nell made a face at him. "Not a bad idea. I don't recall ever getting any sarcasm from a horse."

Howard and Rob each loaded a horse onto the trailer, and Jack pushed the gate closed behind them.

Nell nudged Rob and drew his attention to Katy who was watching from the shadow of the porch. "Ask her to go," she whispered.

Rob walked so slowly over to the porch, anybody would have thought he was saddle sore. "Take a ride?" he asked Katy abruptly.

She was surprised. Was he really asking her to come along? "I have to work on my essay," she said softly.

"It's up to you." Rob shrugged.

He really meant it! Katy jumped off the porch with a whoop and holler and dove into the cab.

"We'll be back for dinner," Rob told Nell.

As they traveled along the highway to Casper, they passed new housing developments and strip malls. They drove past hobby farms with their manicured lawns and shiny clean barns that seemed to have never experienced manure.

They turned left, under a ranch sign that read U-TOPIA, and rolled down the long gravel driveway. Howard was the first to spot Miranda, the girl who had given Katy a bandana for him at the end of the term. She was looking more beautiful than ever in her new cowgirl shirt and boots. She was waving them down a smaller road to the stables.

Rob jumped out of the cab and shook hands with Miranda's father, Rick.

"Esther went shopping with her interior decorator," said Rick, apologizing for his wife's absence. "At this point it'd be cheaper to adopt that lady," joked Rick.

Rob followed him to their sprawling mansion.

Howard walked one of the quarter horses down the ramp toward Miranda.

She smiled and took the lead line. "Hey, handsome."

"Um, thanks," said Howard. "But what do you think about the horse?"

They both giggled and led the horse into the stable.

Katy could see them inside through the open doors. Howard stroked the horse's neck. His hand, with the bandana around the wrist, brushed against Miranda's.

Katy decided to leave the two lovebirds alone.

Miranda brought out the saddle soap and tossed Howard a cloth. They sat down on opposite sides of her saddle and began to polish.

"It needs another coat," said Miranda.

"Yes, ma'am," said Howard in a sassy tone.

"Teamwork is everyone doing exactly what I say," teased Miranda.

"I figured that out already." Howard chuckled.

They worked quietly for a while. Then Miranda asked the most important question on her mind: "Did you tell them?"

Howard didn't need to ask what she meant. "I will. I'm waiting for the right time."

"When is there ever going to be a right time?" asked Miranda. "Just tell them the truth: 'I changed my mind. I'm going to take that scholarship. *Adios muchachos.*' End of discussion."

"Easier said than done."

She shook her head, flapped her elbows up and down, and clucked like a chicken. Howard caught her by the waist and swung her around until they tumbled onto a big pile of hay.

"I feel like a cartoon. . . . My feet are running, but I'm not moving," he confessed.

Miranda laid her hand on his cheek. "I think everyone writes a story in their head that becomes their life. And if you don't write it yourself, somebody else writes it for you."

"That's not going to happen to *my* story," said Howard.

She shimmied up closer to him. "Am *I* in your story?"

In the house, Rick settled down in his King Ranch chair behind a polished mahogany desk and opened up a leather-bound checkbook.

Rob examined a series of historic photos on the wall. Katy peeked her head in the doorway, and Rick waved her in. The photos caught her attention, too. They were from the 1950s when all the land around Casper was still open ranch land.

"This used to be the Chapman ranch," Rick explained. "Twelve thousand acres. Four tough brothers."

"What happened to them?" asked Katy.

Rick handed Rob the check for the horses. "None of the

grandkids wanted to work that hard. Last piece of the property was sold two years ago."

Katy tried to absorb the idea. "You mean they just left?"

"With a great deal of money in their pockets," said Rick. "Our marketing people did a magnificent job. If you're ever curious . . ."

"I'm curious now," said Rob.

Rick went to his desk and pulled one of his glossy real estate development brochures out of a drawer. The front showed a huge new vacation home with a perfect-looking, well-dressed family posing in front.

"How many acres you got, Rob? Five thousand, more or less?" asked Rick.

"Mostly less," replied Rob.

"You could get twenty spectacular home sites out of your ranch, keep your house, and a hundred acres," declared Rick.

Katy was confused. "We can't graze our herd on a hundred acres!" she cried.

"Everything changes in this life, Katy," said Rick. "One

day, some lucky guy's going to marry you. What are you gonna do if he doesn't want to ranch?"

"Break off the engagement," said Katy sarcastically. She figured she knew how to put up with this kind of teasing.

"Wait 'til you fall in love," Rick persisted.

Katy shrugged. "I guess I won't fall in love."

She looked at her dad in all seriousness. "You wouldn't really sell our ranch, would you?"

"Alright, Katy. Don't get all worked up," said Rob.

"But we wouldn't sell," she declared. "We're not like them!" She tossed the brochure back onto Rick's desk.

Rick decided he had hit a nerve and backed off.

"Time to go," Rob told her firmly. "Get in the truck."

She rushed out, and Rob apologized to Rick.

But Rick was contrite. "My fault. You can't tease kids with affection. All they hear is the tease."

Katy stormed back to the truck, confused by the depth of her fear and resentment. She glowered silently as Rick and her father walked out of the house together.

Rick swung their trailer gate closed. "Esther will kill me if

I don't at least *try* to get you to stay for dinner," he said.

"Another time," replied Rob. "Howard! Let's go!"

Howard came out of the barn with Miranda. "I thought we were going to hang out," he said.

"When I have time to 'hang out,' you'll be the first to know," snapped Rob.

Miranda could sense the tension in the air, and tried to lighten the mood. "Hey, guys, I don't know if you're going to the rodeo, but I'm competing in the barrel race again."

"Don't be fooled by that sweet smile," said Rick proudly. "My daughter goes for the jugular when she's competing."

Rob sensed Howard's chagrin and softened a bit. "Sure, we'll go. I don't know anybody who would want to miss that," he said as he climbed into the cab.

Miranda touched Howard's arm. "See you sooner than later."

CHAPTER NINE

As they drove down the highway out of Casper, dark thunderclouds rolled in overhead. But the mood in the truck was even darker.

"You didn't tell us you were gonna sell the ranch." Katy was fuming.

"I'm not discussing it," declared Rob.

Howard looked at his father in surprise. "You are?"

"I was just *talking* to the man," Rob said.

"I guess it can't hurt," said Howard. "I mean, just to explore all your options."

"Yeah, all my options," said Rob sarcastically. He couldn't imagine any options other than "starve on the ranch" or "sell out."

"You'd give our land to strangers?" demanded Katy.

"Katy!" Rob growled.

"It's crazy," she cried. "You know . . . *loco!*"

"Enough!" Rob turned on the radio to put a stop to any further conversation. It was a long ride home.

When they finally arrived, Nell stepped out on the porch to greet them. Katy blew right past her mother and stormed through the kitchen door.

"How'd it go, honey?" asked Nell.

But Katy was already stomping up the stairs to her room.

Nell cringed as she heard her daughter's bedroom door slam shut.

Then Rob strode past her, as silent and fuming as Katy.

"Rob?" Nell tried. She cringed again as he slammed the door to the mudroom.

"Prodigious day, Mom," cried Howard with a big smile

on his face. He gave his mother a hug and a kiss, and bounded up the stairs two at a time.

Nell figured she would hear what happened soon enough. She shook her head, put on her reading glasses, and went back to her desk to finish up the ranch accounting.

Howard was in his room reading when Katy dragged herself in and plopped down on the foot of his bed. She looked around at his walls. They were completely bare. "What happened to your movie posters?" she asked.

"I'm moving into my Zen phase," quipped Howard.

Katy considered this for a moment, and it dawned on her what the blank walls really meant. She wondered if he had said anything to their father yet. "I hate him," she declared.

"Tonight you do," said Howard.

"He'll never know who I really am," she cried.

Howard could see how much she hurt. He took her hand gently. "I know."

Katy looked up at him. "You're going away."

"I'm changing time zones, not solar systems," he said.

"Once you're gone, you'll never come back." She could feel the tears welling up in her eyes.

Howard held her close, knowing that, in a way, she was right. After he left, the ranch would no longer be his home— he would always be a visitor.

That night, Katy went out to Flicka, as usual. This time, the horse cried out in excitement when she saw her.

"Shhhhh," said Katy.

Flicka snorted and stepped closer.

"You came to *me*," she whispered. "You were waiting for *me*."

Very gently, she grabbed hold of Flicka's mane and pulled herself up onto the filly's back. They walked slowly, once around the paddock under the silvery moon. Katy waited for the wild bucking to begin. But Flicka walked steadily and easily.

"Thank you." Katy sighed. She tapped her heels against Flicka's sides and eased her into a trot.

"Wait 'til he sees you," she cried.

Feeling brave, Katy squeezed her heels against Flicka's sides once again. The proud filly began to canter. Flicka was getting it. Katy smiled triumphantly. She had tamed this wild mustang—something her father said she couldn't do!

"Let's go," she whispered. She pulled the rope that released the gate. But Flicka shied at the unfamiliar motion.

Katy leaned forward and sang her soft, coaxing song in Flicka's ear. "You're not scared of that silly old gate. . . . You want to get out of this little pen."

Finally Flicka calmed down and stepped through. Within minutes, horse and rider were cantering across the wide-open pasture as perfectly as Katy had always imagined it would be.

But as Katy was walking Flicka back into the paddock, Rocket, one of the feistiest mares on the ranch, caught Flicka's eye. The mare gave out a sharp whinny. Flicka whinnied back in anger.

"Easy, girl. Let her be," coaxed Katy.

She slowly moved Flicka away from the fence. But several other horses came trotting over to see what the commotion was all about. Soon they were running back and forth tauntingly along the fence adjacent to the paddock. Flicka sidestepped, infuriated and ready to charge.

"No, girl," said Katy. She tried to turn Flicka's head away from the commotion. But Flicka put her head down and bolted.

"No, Flicka!" Katy shouted. She held on for dear life.

Jack and Gus heard the ruckus and came out to see what was wrong. Just as they reached the paddock, Flicka crashed through the fence and leaped into the pasture. Katy went flying and landed hard on her back. Flicka and Rocket bit and snapped at each other furiously, until Flicka finally galloped off with half the herd behind her.

Rob and Nell emerged from the house and raced toward Katy. Howard flew out the door just a few steps behind them. By the time they reached her, she was sitting up, stunned and aching.

"Are you hurt?" asked Rob.

She kept her eyes fixed on the ground. "No."

Nell dabbed away the blood on her daughter's chin. She knew that any other girl would be crying by now.

Jack and Gus tossed their lariats around Flicka's neck and used their ropes to try to subdue her. The mustang struggled violently.

Rob watched them for a moment, then looked back at Katy. "You couldn't *plan* a better way to get yourself killed."

"Rob, don't," pleaded Nell.

"Don't *what*?" Rob shouted. "Be her father? You're not protecting her. You're *crippling* her. She's going to end up as useless as that mustang."

Nell set her hand on Howard's shoulder, warning him to keep out of it.

"Flicka isn't useless," cried Katy. "She wants to learn."

Rob wheeled around toward her menacingly. "No, she doesn't. You want something that doesn't exist . . . an animal wild as the wind but loyal to you. Well, she's neither. She'd die on her own, but she can't be broken. It's time you see her for what she is."

"I know what she is," said Katy.

"How do you know *anything* about that creature?" demanded Rob.

"Because we're the same!" cried Katy.

This caught Rob by surprise. His worst fear had come true—she must have been working with the wild horse against his orders. "I won't have her on my ranch," he declared.

"But . . . Daddy, please!" Katy begged.

"You did this behind my back," he cried.

Katy could see the hurt and frustration in his face.

"I know she's sorry about what happened," offered Nell.

"Don't make excuses for her," said Rob. "It's the same as if she lied to my face."

"You don't get it," Katy cried. "You don't get *anything*!" She fled to the house in a fury.

Howard just glared at his father, shook his head, and went after his sister.

Nell stood by Rob's side trying to summon the willpower to speak her mind. "There's got to be a better way. . . ."

Rob cut her off. "If there is, I don't know it," he declared, and he stormed off to the barn.

CHAPTER TEN

The dazzling July sun lit up the snowy peaks of the Neversummer Mountains, and a sharp wind blew down into the valley the day Norbert Rye drove his big livestock trailer down the gravel road to the Goose Creek Ranch.

He pulled up at the paddock, and Rob helped him slide the ramp down from the back of his trailer. Jack and Gus roped Flicka, struggled to guide her up the ramp, and closed the trailer door behind her.

Katy came tearing around the barn and charged toward Norbert like a wild mustang. "No! You can't take her!!"

Norbert looked to Rob for his decision.

"Katy," said Rob. "It's better this way."

As if to prove Rob right, Flicka kicked hard against the walls of the trailer.

"She's never been in a trailer before," cried Katy.

"She'll be fine, sweetie," said Norbert. "She's gonna be a rodeo star."

"She's scared." Katy imagined exactly how she would feel if she were locked up like that. "She can't see the sky."

Rob looked at Nell, hoping she would say something—anything to get them through this impasse. But Nell refused to help.

Katy rushed past him and tried to open the trailer's gate.

Rob pulled her back. "Stop it."

She turned on him in a fury, fists flying. He tried to hold her back, but one punch landed on his chest with a dull thud.

"Katy, please." He desperately tried to hold her, to calm her down.

"You're not my father anymore!" she shouted.

Rob let her go. He was stung to the quick by her words. But he would not budge from his decision.

"Flicka should stay," said Howard.

"Stay out of this," cried Rob.

"I'll help Katy take care of her," Howard offered.

"Is that right? You have the money to buy her back?" asked Rob.

"I do," said Nell. "I have some money saved. On my own."

He glared at her in disbelief. "What is wrong with you?"

"Not a thing," cried Nell. "You made this decision without me. Because you know it's wrong. Now here's another decision for you: Unload Flicka . . . before you look like a fool."

Katy looked on, speechless. She had never seen her parents fighting in public this way.

"I'm done discussing this," declared Rob.

"I'm not," said Howard, gathering his courage. "Katy found Flicka. She should decide."

"Until you're running this ranch, I'll make the decisions."

"I don't want to run your ranch," declared Howard.

After a year at boarding school, Katy McLaughlin is happy to be home for the summer.

Always looking for adventure, Katy tries to capture a wild mustang.

It doesn't work out *quite* as well as she planned.

Katy's father finally ropes the wild horse.

Katy names her horse "Flicka."

Watch out! Runaway horse!

Alone in the mountains,
Katy attempts to
find her way home.

Flicka tries to save Katy from a mountain lion.

It may be too late for Flicka . . .

. . . but is it too late for Katy?

Rob shot Nell an accusing glance. But Nell was as shocked as he was.

"I'm sick of this place," Howard finally confessed. "I've given it a lot of thought, and guess what—I'm never going to be a rancher. I want to go to college."

Nell couldn't believe her ears. "Why haven't you said anything?"

"Because this was what you wanted me to do. Katy wants this ranch. I don't want any part of it."

Rob was reeling, but he tried to hide his dismay. "I'm sorry you feel that way," he said flatly. He turned to the rodeo entrepreneur. "Norbert, take your horse away."

Norbert couldn't wait to be off. "Hope to see you folks at the fairgrounds," he said. He tipped his hat politely and hurried into his rig.

Katy sprinted after him shouting. She could hear Flicka inside whinnying and kicking the walls.

When the trailer had disappeared in the distance, Katy ran through the pasture and the meadows until her heart and lungs were bursting. She ran as wild and free as she knew

Flicka would have wanted to be. But her friend was not free—her father had sold her into bondage, to be a moment's entertainment for the anonymous rodeo crowds.

Exhausted, Katy finally slunk back into the house, where her father ordered her to her bedroom. She slipped into the chair behind her desk. She imagined the herd of wild mustangs from her favorite painting coming to life again. She opened her test booklet and picked up her pencil.

"Sometimes when the light disappears, an afterimage remains . . . but just for a moment. Mustangs are an afterimage of the west. No better than ghosts. Hardly there at all. No one really wants them. Not ranchers, not city people. That's their real destiny: Let them disappear—once and for all, along with all the other misfits, loners, and relics of a wilderness no one cares about anymore."

Katy imagined the Wyoming prairie, vast and empty. She wrote and wrote, her eyes wet with fury.

A few days later, Howard found her in her room, sitting listlessly, writing at her desk.

"Want to go swimming?" he asked.

"No thanks," she replied.

"It's a thousand degrees in here," said Howard.

Katy scowled. "I'm busy."

"I can tell." Howard moved closer and looked over her shoulder. "You *really* want to go swimming."

"What's *he* going to say?" she asked.

"That's *his* problem," said Howard. "Let me see if mom is home."

Howard bounded down the stairs to the kitchen, where Nell was catching up with some sewing. He gave her a conspiratorial look. "Mom must've gone to town!" he shouted up to Katy. "So stop making excuses and come swimming!"

Howard gently coaxed his mom to hide in the pantry.

"Good move," whispered Nell.

"I know," said Howard.

She kissed his brow and he hurried out to meet Katy.

Katy looked around the kitchen suspiciously. "You sure about this?"

"We'll be back before anybody even knows," Howard reassured her. "I'm hot. You hot?"

"Yeah," cried Katy.

"Heck, yeah!"

Nell just smiled as she heard the door closing behind them.

CHAPTER ELEVEN

Within minutes, Howard and Katy had gotten Yankee and Chariot out of the barn, and they were racing bareback for the pond. They whooped and galloped at full speed, zigzagging down the rocky canyon like a couple of daredevils. They kept racing until they splashed straight into the pond. The moment the horses were up to their bellies in the water, Katy and Howard dove in.

Katy popped to the surface like an otter. She looked around for Howard, but, to her surprise, the first person she saw was Miranda!

"Close your eyes, cowgirl," cried Miranda.

Howard popped up right next to Katy and splashed her in the face. Katy splashed back harder.

"Okay, I surrender!" Howard laughed.

But he stopped teasing abruptly, and he and Miranda exchanged a serious look.

"What's going on?" asked Katy.

Miranda and Howard hesitated, trying to decide who was going to speak first.

"*Somebody* tell me," Katy cried.

"Miranda saw Flicka," said Howard.

Katy looked at Miranda, desperate to hear news—any news. "Where?"

"At the fairgrounds," said Miranda. "When I was practicing the course."

"How did she look?" asked Katy.

Miranda checked with Howard.

Katy could see she was agonizing about something. "What?" she cried.

Miranda took a deep breath. "I've never ever been scared around horses. Not in my entire life. But those horses Flicka was with . . ." She paused, afraid to give voice to what she was thinking.

"Don't stop!" cried Katy.

Miranda spoke softly. "You'd have to really work at it to make horses that angry."

Katy flipped over on her back and let the water hold her up.

"I'm sorry, Katy," said Howard. "I just thought you'd want to know."

"It's okay," Katy whispered.

They floated together in the cool water of the pond, watching the pure white clouds moving across the deep azure sky like a herd of wild mustangs.

"They say the purse is eight thousand dollars," said Miranda as a kind of afterthought.

Something lit up in Katy's mind. She dove under and came up right in front of Howard. "I can win that race," she declared.

"My demented sister is even more demented than I thought," quipped Howard.

"Riders get to choose their horses, right?" Katy asked, getting even more excited.

"Yeah," said Miranda.

"I choose Flicka. I win."

"If you can stay on her," said Miranda.

"I can."

"You're too young to enter," Howard reminded her.

"*You're* not," cried Katy.

Howard blanched. "Bad idea."

"Brilliant idea," cried Katy. "I buy Flicka back with the prize money." She slapped the water triumphantly. "She won't be Dad's horse anymore. She'll be *mine*. And if she wins, someone will want her foal. That's money in my pocket. And I swear, if he tries to sell our land, I'll buy that, too!"

Howard grabbed Katy and tried to settle her down. "Katy, she's way too dangerous to ride."

"Maybe for *you*, but not for me," said Katy. "You've only got to stay on her a few seconds. I've already done that." She looked to Miranda for approval.

Suddenly Miranda broke into a wide smile and raised her

arm to show her "yea" vote.

"The people have spoken," cried Katy.

"No," said Howard, "the inmates have taken over the asylum."

Katy swam closer. "C'mon," she coaxed, "let's see you walk it like you talk it."

Howard flopped back in the water and held up his arms in defeat.

Katy hugged him and kissed his cheek.

"Drown me, please," he said with a playful smirk.

Katy could see the whole event in her mind, just as she could imagine the wild mustangs coming to life in her favorite painting. She let out a wild whoop that echoed off the walls of the canyon.

They were quiet for a while when Miranda began to laugh. "I've been waiting a long time for somebody to be a bad influence on me."

Katy smiled. "You're welcome."

Even Howard had to laugh.

CHAPTER TWELVE

After lunch that day, Rob and Jack were out on the range fixing fences when Nell rode up on her big paint horse, leading Rob's gelding along beside her.

The men turned at the sound of the horses approaching and wiped their sweaty brows.

Nell looked at Rob and handed him the reins of his horse. "Don't say anything," she told him. "Get on."

Jack could see that Nell had something urgent on her mind. He waved Rob off without a word and went back to the chores by himself.

Nell cantered off to her favorite hilltop, where she and Rob could stop and look out over the whole ranch.

"When the kids were little I'd tuck them in and say, 'I'll love you 'til the mountains tumble down,'" said Nell when they were side by side.

She struggled to find the right words. "Right now it feels like they could blow away any second. . . ."

Rob understood her pain. "Before Dad died, he asked me if I wanted to sell the ranch and take the cash."

Nell had never heard him say this before.

"I said 'over my dead body,'" he continued. "'No way. Not ever.' I thought that's what he wanted me to say. But, no, he seemed almost . . . disappointed. He said he wasn't sure if what he was giving me made sense anymore."

He sighed. "Maybe he was right. One heat wave and a broodmare loses her foal. One gopher hole and a stallion snaps his leg. Sometimes I catch myself and realize . . . I'm *afraid*. . . .

"But then I see those kids hanging out in malls . . . sullen, lazy, no ambition, no dreams . . . This is the only way I know how to save our children."

"Howard doesn't need saving," said Nell. "He'll be fine wherever he goes. But Katy . . . we could lose her. She's smart and she's strong, but she can't survive out there. She doesn't get the way it works. She's not selfish or phony enough."

"My daughter lives in a fantasy land," declared Rob.

"So do you," cried Nell. "You live up on cowboy mountain and let the world pass by below."

"No one forced you to come here," snapped Rob. "I know you miss having people around."

Nell was so frustrated, she roared like an angry lioness. "This is the only place in the world I want to be, and you know it!"

Rob shifted in his saddle.

Nell looked him straight in the eye. "When are you gonna look at your daughter and see she's *you*? And that's why I love her so much. . . ."

Rob took Nell's hand and pressed it gently against his

lips. They sat side by side on their horses, holding hands as the evening sun blazed red on the horizon.

"They want to go to the rodeo," said Nell.

Rob shook his head. "She wants to see Flicka."

He paused for a while. "They expect me to say 'no.'"

Nell waited for his answer.

"Bet I'd blow their minds if I said 'yes.' They'd see how diabolical I can really be."

Nell smiled. "You're such a bad boy. I love it."

Early the next morning, Katy got dressed for the big day. She and Howard were indeed surprised that their father said yes to the rodeo, but Katy also knew in her heart that she would not have taken no for an answer.

She studied herself in the mirror. She slipped on her cowboy hat and tucked her long hair up underneath. She pulled on her leather work gloves and put on a real tough-guy face. Yes . . . she could do this! She nodded and tipped her own hat in approval.

Rob waited behind the wheel of the truck. Jack leaned by the open tailgate in his fancy new cowboy shirt. He reeked of aftershave.

"That smell will scare the livestock," commented Gus, who had decided to stay behind and keep an eye on the ranch.

"Ah, but the ladies find it reassuring. Let's them know I'm sensitive, not just a sexy hunk."

Katy ran up, breathless. "Can we go now?" She paused a moment and sniffed the air. "God, what's that smell?"

Gus guffawed as Katy slipped into the cab, followed by Nell and Howard in his crisp white shirt and new Levi's.

Rob adjusted the rearview mirror as Jack hopped into the flatbed.

"Well, c'mon," cried Katy impatiently.

Rob honked the horn to say so long to Gus, and they tore down the driveway and turned out on the open highway.

CHAPTER THIRTEEN

By the look of the parking lot at the fairgrounds, half the state of Wyoming must've turned out for the rodeo. Rob found a place to park among the thousands of cars and trucks, and they hurried through the gates. The McLaughlins passed the livestock auction, the tractor pull, and the Native American dance show, and went straight into the stands to see the barrel races. Miranda was just beginning her round.

She rode at a swift, smooth pace, weaving gracefully through the barrels. The crowed roared their approval. She made the wide turn at the far end and started back. But she cut one turn a little too close. The crowd oohed.

Howard could see the look of disappointment on Miranda's face as she crossed the finish line. He knew that one little slip could cost her the event.

Rob and Nell decided it would be okay to let the kids enjoy the rodeo on their own for a bit. They synchronized their watches.

"We'll meet you right here at ten," said Rob.

"Ten!?" cried Howard. He looked to his mother for a second opinion.

"Maybe we can sleep in tomorrow," Nell offered.

"The horses don't sleep in," snapped Rob. "Ten o'clock."

"Knock, knock," said Nell.

Rob looked at her as if she'd gone crazy.

"Knock, knock," she repeated.

Rob sighed. "Who's there?"

"Control freak," replied Nell. "Now you say, control freak, who?" She grinned and Howard and Katy burst out laughing.

Rob put on an air of mock dignity. "Actually, your mom and I think midnight is a better idea."

He pulled out his wallet and gave each of them some cash. But knowing the rodeo was a once-a-year treat, Nell dug into her wallet and gave them each some more.

Miranda walked over to where they were standing. "Hey, everybody!"

"How'd you do?" asked Nell.

Miranda sighed. "Fifth place."

"You really looked good out there," said Rob. "The competition was tough this year."

"I heard the wild-horse races are bringing out a different crowd than usual," said Miranda.

Katy realized Miranda was saying this for *her* benefit.

"Those cowboys sure are crazy. My horse got distracted. I did, too," said Miranda.

Katy locked eyes with her and gave her a level stare. There was no way she was backing down! "Let's go."

Howard grabbed Miranda's hand.

She gave him a flirtatious look. "Doesn't he look cute when he's all cleaned up?"

"We're wasting time," grumbled Katy. She grabbed Howard's other hand and pulled him toward Miranda's horse trailer, where they had hidden the riding clothes she would need.

Miranda politely waved good-bye to Rob and Nell, and they headed off in the other direction.

"I mean it. It's like in a second I forgot everything I knew about riding," Miranda told Katy, once the two girls were alone inside the trailer together. "I'm scared for you. . . ."

Katy gritted her teeth in determination. "I'm not," she declared. "Not even a little."

She stepped out of the trailer, and Howard looked her over.

"What do you think?" asked Katy.

"I think I should be the voice of reason," he replied.

"We're running out of time," cried Katy.

"Okay, hold on." Howard scooped up a handful of dirt and smudged it along her upper lip and on her cheeks.

Miranda buttoned Katy's jean jacket all the way up and turned up the collar, until her young face seemed to nearly disappear. Katy tried to swagger confidently, like an old rodeo pro.

Howard got in line at the registration counter. He waited while the clerk in a straw cowboy hat wrote out a receipt for the man in front of him. Suddenly Howard spotted Norbert Rye going into the main office, briefcase and two-way radio in hand. Howard tipped his hat low and turned away. When the office door had closed, Howard turned back to the clerk.

"Can I help you?" he asked impatiently.

"I want to register for an event," said Howard.

The clerk stared at him. "You gonna tell me which one or do I have to read your mind?"

"The wild-horse race," declared Howard.

The clerk scowled. "The wild-horse race requires a team of two."

"That's my partner . . . outside." Howard pointed out the door toward Katy, who was trying to look big while hiding behind Miranda at the same time.

"Fifty dollars, a driver's license, and a signed release form," said the clerk.

Howard fished his license and money out of his wallet, hoping this man could not hear how loud and fast his heart was beating.

The clerk slapped two rodeo number cards on the table. Howard and Katy would be team number fourteen.

"Report to the corral to select your horse. Event rolls at five PM sharp!" The clerk grinned sadistically. "And if you come to your senses and want to back out . . . you lose every penny."

CHAPTER FOURTEEN

When they reached the corral, they saw Flicka, wide-eyed and agitated, standing amid thirty other wild mustangs. A gray mare nipped at Flicka, and she flew into a screaming, kicking, biting fury. The cowboys looked on, amazed.

Katy climbed the fence and watched Flicka being pursued by several other horses. She was so upset she jumped right down into the corral.

The director of the event saw her. "Hey!" he shouted. "Get outta there, you lunatic!"

The other teams, busy helping each other pin their numbers on, turned and laughed at her.

Howard helped her back over the fence.

The director walked up to her menacingly. "You choose your horse like everybody else. Or you take a hike." He turned to the other riders. "Now gather up!"

There were more than a dozen teams, with contestants that ranged from teenagers to thirty-year-olds. Most looked nervous, but the rider on team number six looked particularly cocky.

He smirked at Katy. "Rules say you can put a baby cradle on the horse?"

The other teams chuckled. Katy kept her eyes fixed on the ground, refusing to give in to any intimidation.

"Quiet. Okay. Shout 'em out!" cried the director.

The riders hurried to the fence and called out their choices. "We'll take that chestnut! . . . The blaze! . . . Black with the star! . . . We got the paint!" And the director noted them on his clipboard.

Katy nudged Howard. "We'll take the black filly!" he called.

The director paused and looked up from his notes. "Son, you just lost this race," he commented. "That horse is truly loco." He finished recording everyone's choices and addressed the teams. "Boys: Next time you see your horses, they'll be loose in the ring trying to run you over. Good luck!"

As the afternoon progressed, the fairgrounds were bathed in a warm, golden light. The twang of rock and country bands drifted out from the bandstand and from the various dance pavilions. It was time for eating corn dogs and fried dough. Time to try out the Ferris wheel and the roller coaster or, like Nell and Rob, to have a slow dance with your sweetheart and then go for a stroll down the fairway.

Rob took a bite from an enormous ball of blue cotton candy.

"Ugh," said Nell. "Why do you eat that junk?"

Rob stuck out his bright-blue tongue. "It makes me sweeter."

Nell laughed.

Rob spotted a familiar couple, in matching western attire, walking toward them down the fairway.

Rick and Esther Koop's faces lit up when they saw Nell and Rob. "Honey, it's our future in-laws," drawled Rick.

"I don't think these lovely people deserve to go bankrupt 'cause our daughter marries into their family," teased Esther.

Nell and Esther laughed and exchanged a friendly hug.

"Has anyone seen them?" asked Nell.

"Miranda has superpowers," said Esther. "When she wants to ditch us she becomes invisible."

"Teenagers who don't want to hang out with their parents? Where did we go wrong?" joked Rick.

"So, what's next?" asked Rob. "Tilt-A-Whirl? Haunted Castle? Or maybe the Stagecoach of Love?"

Back in the wild-horse corral, the kids had more serious business on their minds. Miranda carefully pinned Katy and Howard's numbers on the backs of their shirts. They could hear the noise of the crowd that had gathered and a few muddy-sounding announcements coming over the P.A. system.

Howard was hit with a bad case of the jitters. "Can we rethink this?"

"You think too much," declared Katy.

Miranda looked truly upset. "But what if—"

"If you don't want to do it, I'll do it myself," Katy interrupted her.

"Calm down," said Howard. "You don't have to make everything a loyalty test."

"Everything *is*," she scowled.

"Ladies, gentlemen . . . and cowboys!" cried the announcer on the P.A. system. "The wild-horse race is about to start. If you've got a weak heart, if you faint easy, or if you just ate a big meal . . . enter at your own risk!"

The crowd cheered wildly.

"Let's go," said Katy.

The lights were on over the ring, and the teams gathered at the chutes.

Howard held Miranda's saddle.

"Thanks for letting me use your saddle," said Katy.

Miranda gave her a warm, sisterly hug. "Go kick some cowboy ass!"

Howard reached out to give her a hug, too, but Miranda pulled him close and kissed him. "Don't you dare get hurt," she whispered.

But Katy had spotted someone staring in their direction. "Rats!"

It was Norbert Rye coming down the steps toward them.

Howard and Katy pulled their hats low and turned away from him. He breezed right past them, and they breathed a sigh of relief as they crowded in with the other teams.

"Do you think he recognized us?" asked Katy.

"Don't know," replied Howard.

"Hey folks!" cried the announcer. What do ya call a thousand pounds of smelly, rowdy, empty-headed, food-guzzling fury? Oh, you've met my brother-in-law. Okay, now direct your attention to the hold. That ain't an earthquake beneath your feet! That's wild horses comin' at ya!"

The horses each had a number hanging around its neck now, and they were being driven into their chutes.

"Look at those crazy devils!" cried the announcer. "Never saddled, never haltered—angrier than a cowboy who just totaled his pickup!"

The crowd whooped and hollered.

"Anybody who'd get on one of those beasts can't be too smart. In fact, these boys are so dumb they'd call four one one to get the number for nine one one."

Each rider tried to concentrate on the task at hand, their hearts racing.

"By the way, folks, those ain't rodeo clowns you see wearin' them funny clothes. Those are just medics with a sense of humor. So let's all throw a good-bye kiss to these cowboys. This might be the last time we see them vertical."

The spectators all blew exaggerated kisses to the riders.

Number six grinned over his saddle at Katy. "This race is mine. So watch your back, girlie."

Katy whispered to Howard. "He said 'girlie.'"

"He's joking. Relax," said Howard.

The announcer continued his introduction. "In a few moments the horses will be released. All at once."

The crowd went wild.

Katy imagined what it would feel like to be one of the gladiators thrown into a Roman coliseum.

"These boys got to grab 'em, saddle 'em, then ride 'em between that pair of barrels," the announcer explained. "Any rider who can stay on that long wins eight thousand dollars! So . . . let's bring out the first set of victims. . . . I mean cowboys!"

Katy, Howard, and Miranda watched as the first group of contestants marched out into the ring.

"Ten seconds, folks! Let's count it down together," cried the announcer.

"Ten, nine, eight, seven . . . " the crowd shouted.

The riders braced themselves.

" . . . six, five, four, three, two, one!"

The director threw open the gates to the chutes. Two rodeo cowboys banged sticks against the rail fence, and the wild horses charged out. Howard and Katy couldn't believe how fast everything was happening. The first team reached their horse, but the horse jerked its head up, and the rider couldn't catch the lead. The team two rider dropped his saddle and was knocked down while trying to pick it up. Rider number five was one foot in the stirrup, about to swing his other leg over when his horse bumped him into the wooden fence that surrounded the ring. Finally rider eight managed to mount his steed, but just as he turned his horse toward the barrels, the horse threw him down into the dirt and kicked him hard.

Howard could not believe the utter chaos in the ring. "No way," he told Katy.

"What?" she cried.

"Are you friggin' crazy?"

She glowered at him. "Try and stop me."

The bell announcing the end of the round rang, and a roar went up from the crowd. Rodeo workers herded the horses back out of the ring. Medics rushed in to assist the riders who had been injured, and the rest limped out on their own.

"Let's hear it for the winners!" cried the announcer. "Well, I'll be darned. . . . We don't have any! Okay, I'd score it . . . horses one, cowboys zero!"

Katy and Howard stopped arguing as a rodeo worker walked by. "Your group is next," he warned.

Once he was gone, Howard grabbed Katy. "I'm giving back my number," he declared.

"Go ahead," she said. She locked her arms around the saddle and pulled it away from him.

"Know what we say to our next group of cowboys? Welcome to our nightmare! Let's bring 'em in!" cried the announcer.

The gate opened and Katy stepped into the ring ahead of everyone. Howard swore under his breath and rushed in after her.

As the audience shouted out the countdown for the second time, Katy began to feel cold and dizzy with anticipation.

". . . six, five, four, three, two, one!"

Howard rested his hand on her shoulder, still trying to talk her out of the ring. But by now the roar of the crowd was so loud, she couldn't hear a word he was saying.

The chutes slid open. Horses charged past them from every direction. For a moment Katy stood still, overwhelmed by the chaos. Rider number six shoved her out of the way and bounded past.

She recovered her balance. "There!" she cried pointing at Flicka. Katy ran toward her. She spread her arms open and Flicka seemed to recognize the signal. She slowed down and seemed to want to approach.

"It's me, girl," said Katy.

Katy eased closer, with Howard stepping close behind her.

"Give me the lead," she said.

Just as Howard handed Katy the lead, a big paint bumped into her. She stumbled, and Flicka tore off.

"Flicka!" she called.

Flicka stopped again and turned.

"Easy, Flicka," she coaxed. "I'm here to help you."

"Keep talking to her," urged Howard.

"You know me. I'm your friend, Katy." She began singing the soothing song Flicka had grown accustomed to during their early-morning hours together in the paddock at home.

Flicka stood still and watched her intently.

"What a good girl," said Katy.

Suddenly Flicka reared up.

Howard jumped back, but Katy stood her ground. Flicka's hooves came down right in front of her. The wild mustang grew calm and nickered gently. Katy rested her head gently against Flicka's. "I'll set you free."

Katy turned and smiled at her brother. All of Howard's doubts evaporated in that instant. He knew he would do everything he could to help her.

CHAPTER FIFTEEN

But at that same moment, even deeper troubles were beginning for Howard and Katy. Norbert ran into Rob, Nell, Rick, and Esther just outside the stands. He gave Rob a big, knowing grin. "Guess you changed your mind about mustangs, didn't ya?"

Rob had no idea what Norbert was talking about. "Come again?"

Now Norbert was confused. "You're here to see your boy ride that wild horse, right?"

"My boy?"

"Where is he?!" cried Nell.

"Follow me," said Norbert.

They walked toward the main arena.

Once inside, Norbert led the McLaughlins and the Koops to the VIP section in the stands. Rob and Nell stood on tiptoe surveying the scary scene in the ring, hoping to get a glimpse of Howard.

"I see him," cried Rob.

"Who's that with him?" asked Esther.

Nell was the first to see. "Oh, God. . . . It's Katy."

Without a moment's hesitation Rob vaulted over the fence and dropped into the ring.

Katy had managed to slip the lead over Flicka's head, and Howard was holding her steady for the saddle.

"Keep her still!" cried Katy.

Howard lifted the saddle, but the motion spooked Flicka, and she knocked it to the ground. Katy bent over and lifted it slowly.

As Howard glanced up to the stands, he saw their father entering the ring. "Oh, God. He's here."

Katy looked over her shoulder and saw Rob moving carefully along the perimeter of the ring looking for them.

Katy was overcome with sorrow. "I'm an idiot," she declared. "He'll never let me keep Flicka."

Howard was surprised by the sudden hopelessness in her voice. "Just win!" he cried.

"It won't make any difference to him. He doesn't want either of us." She dropped the saddle on the ground, grabbed a fistful of Flicka's mane, and leaped on bareback.

"Katy, wait!" cried Howard.

He tried to go after her, but rider number six, finally astride the big paint, came bucking and spinning between them. The paint's antics spooked Flicka, and she charged off with Katy astride her.

Howard chased after them. Rob stopped in his tracks, helplessly watching them speed away.

"Ladies and gentlemen," cried the announcer, "this is an

emergency announcement: Does anyone here have a straightjacket? 'Cause it looks like one of our boys is riding bareback!"

Katy bent low over Flicka's shoulders and neck, gripped hard with her legs, and anchored her hands in Flicka's mane.

Back in the VIP seats, Nell turned to Norbert. "Stop it!" she demanded with great vehemence.

"How am I gonna do that?" he asked helplessly.

She loomed in his face with the ferocity of a lioness protecting her cubs. "Quickly. And *now*!"

"I'll do what I can," he said respectfully.

Katy leaned down against Flicka's neck to pick up her lead line. One of the other horses swiped past her at full tilt, nearly knocking her off. She recovered and tried again. This time she reached the line and she pulled Flicka around.

The paint bucked crazily, throwing rider number six to the dusty ground. Not one other rider had managed to stay on their mounts.

Katy turned Flicka toward the barrels. She urged the

filly forward. "Run, girl!"

Rob sprinted off after her. Jack spotted Rob in the ring and jumped in to help.

Katy and Flicka galloped toward the barrels. By now the audience was shouting like a horde of lunatics. It really looked as if this crazy young cowboy was going to make it!

Up in the stands, Norbert returned and reassured Nell. "Don't worry, we're gonna get your boy off safely."

"That's not my son," said Nell. "It's my *daughter*."

"Your *girl*?" cried Norbert. "Dear God . . ."

Katy and Flicka rocketed between the barrels.

Norbert's cowboys waved their hats, but Katy just blew on past them. Howard and Rob motioned for her to stop. But she flew past them as well.

In the full wave of the adrenaline rush, she gritted her teeth and kicked her heels against Flicka's sides. "I won't let them take us, girl!" she cried. At her command, Flicka accelerated to terrifying speed and thundered through the gates and out of the ring.

"What's this kid doing!?" cried Norbert.

Howard signaled desperately for Katy to pull up. But she ignored him, tearing out through the parking lot, past the startled rodeo patrons, down a long aisle of parked pickups and vans, and out the back exit.

Rob and Jack and Howard stood by helplessly, watching Katy and Flicka disappear into the darkness of the night.

CHAPTER SIXTEEN

Norbert flipped open his cell phone, called the police, and requested a search party. Within minutes, Wyoming state troopers were speeding out toward the foothills where Katy had vanished. Soon they were combing the countryside looking for her.

The troopers had parked side by side at the end of a long dirt road that led into the foothills of the Neversummer Mountains, and the flashing red lights of their cars cut through the deep Wyoming darkness. The McLaughlins and the Koops drove up to where the rescue party was parked, and hurried to meet the officers. They just shook their heads in frustration. They had not seen any sign of Katy or the horse in the hour they'd been searching.

Howard and Miranda huddled forlornly on the McLaughlin's tailgate, and Esther wrapped herself in a blanket to ward off the chill of the night.

Rick made a series of desperate phone calls. Finally he flapped his cell phone shut and walked over to Rob. "I can't get a helicopter up 'til morning." He sighed.

They heard a low rumble of thunder, and looked up anxiously at the sky. A storm was moving in quickly.

They spotted Norbert walking down out of the foothills.

"The boys lost her trail," he puffed. "Probably won't be able to pick up anything 'til daylight."

"Norbert," said Rob, "give me a horse."

"Two horses," said Nell.

"Calm down," said Norbert.

"We'll calm down when we find our daughter—" cried Nell.

Howard interrupted them. "She'll go home."

"She won't be able to find her way," said Nell. "Not in the mountains . . . in the dark."

"Not Katy," said Howard. "*Flicka*. Our mountains are her home, too."

Rob locked eyes with his son. "I think you're right. We'll ride out as soon as we get back."

A sharp gust of wind swooped across the valley where they were parked, and blew the cowboy hat right off Norbert's head. "Weather's movin' in," he said as he caught the hat in midair.

Rob, Nell, Jack, and Howard hurried into their truck and sped home. They would search for Katy from there while the others continued their search on this side.

With lightning casting a ghostly, flickering light on the inky horizon, Katy and Flicka made their way down a rocky slope. They were on a narrow trail leading into the valley toward the Goose Creek Ranch. Cold rain was blowing in slant-wise on the fierce wind.

The trail took them down a steep bank to the edge of Goose Creek. The usually quiet stream was now gushing full-force from the rain falling in the mountains. They stopped by the stream and Flicka whinnied.

"This is our creek, isn't it?" asked Katy. "Good girl. If we cross to the low bank, we can just follow it home." She paused for a moment and imagined what her father's reaction would be when he saw them.

"He's going to be really angry at us. But we showed him!"

Flicka shook her head, startled.

"What is it, girl?" Katy leaned forward and listened.

There was a low, sad noise, like the sound of someone crying. Katy peered into the darkness. Suddenly the murmur rounded out into a full rumbling growl.

Katy looked up to the top of the bank they had just walked down. A pair of yellow eyes glinted at her. She heard the growl again.

A flash of lightning revealed it for an instant—the mountain lion! As an explosion of thunder boomed, the big cat vanished. Katy turned Flicka toward the creek. They would cross it and be out of danger.

Flicka shied away from the water. They heard another growl, close enough this time to make Katy shiver in fright. Another lightning flash revealed the lion crouched on a branch right above them. Flicka bolted forward, and the sudden motion threw Katy off. As she came down hard on the rocks beside the stream, the lion pounced on Flicka's back and dug its teeth into her neck. Flicka reared and fell to the ground, the lion still clinging to her flesh. Katy scrambled to her feet and shouted, *"FLICKA!!"* She began throwing rocks at the big cat. *"Get away!!!!"*

The flurry of rocks frightened the cat, but Flicka was badly hurt.

Katy sank to her knees in despair. "Get up, Flicka," she cried.

Flicka tried to lift her head, but her wounds were too deep.

"You can't stay here," pleaded Katy. "That lion is gonna come back."

Flicka refused to move. Katy sat close to Flicka in the rain and cradled her head in her arms.

"Hey! Somebody! Help me!! Please!!!" Katy yelled in desperation. She knew it was no use—she was much too far away for anyone to hear her.

CHAPTER SEVENTEEN

As soon as they arrived at the ranch, Howard shouted the news to Gus, and he threw open the barn doors for them. Jack and Rob put on their rain slickers and saddled their horses. Nell grabbed her slicker and began saddling her horse, too.

"You should stay here," said Rob.

"Like nothing I should," cried Nell.

"I'm coming, too," declared Howard.

"Someone should stay," said Rob.

"I'll wait for her," said Gus.

Nell was the first one out. Rob, Jack, and Howard hurried

to catch up.

They turned on their bright flashlights, hitched them to their saddle horns, spread out, and began to search the hills and canyons.

Suddenly Rob rode up right beside Nell. "I'm going to check the creek," he shouted over the roar of the wind and rain. "You should turn back."

Nell was wet and cold and shivering, but absolutely nothing could have made her head home. She pushed past him shouting, *"KATY!"*

Rob hurried down the slope toward the creek. At the top of the steep bank, he dismounted and led his horse between the rocks and scrub. *"KATY!!"* He maneuvered closer to the water, weaving through the cottonwood trees.

Suddenly he spotted two dark shapes on the ground up ahead. He dropped his horse's reins and ran. It was Katy—holding Flicka to keep her calm, her shirt tied around Flicka's neck to stop the flow of blood. Rob fell to his knees beside them.

"I told you there was a lion," said Katy.

Rob scooped her up into his arms.

"KATY! KATY!!" Rob could hear Nell and Howard shouting over the gusts of wind. He cradled his limp and exhausted daughter under his slicker, put her on his horse, and rode her up the bank, leaving Flicka behind.

Nell and Howard caught sight of them and cantered over.

"She's soaked right through," said Rob.

Katy was shivering violently, her eyes closed.

Nell gasped in dismay.

As they galloped up to the house, Gus rushed out to meet them.

"Is she alright?" he asked.

"I hope so," said Rob. "Go find Jack and tell him we found her."

Nell dried Katy's hair, dressed her in her flannel pajamas, and tucked her into bed. Still she shivered and her eyes looked bleary and glazed.

Rob took her temperature. "One hundred and five

degrees! Can that be right?"

Nell knew they had to act immediately to get the fever down. "Howard," she cried. "Get the ice pack from the freezer."

Katy tossed and turned in feverish delirium, seeing the mountain lion pouncing again and again, reliving all the terrible events of the night. *"Flicka . . . Flicka . . ."* she whispered.

Down by Goose Creek, Gus found Jack kneeling beside the wounded filly. Her eyes were wide with terror, her neck and flanks caked with blood.

Flicka whinnied as Gus rubbed his hand along her chest. "She's cut deep," he said.

"We ought to take away her pain," said Jack.

But Gus was uneasy with the idea. "You gonna shoot her?"

Jack shrugged indecisively. "What do you think?"

Back at the house, Rob and Nell decided they had to get Katy to the hospital at once. Rob pulled the truck up next to the porch. Nell wrapped Katy in a big blanket and Rob lifted her into the seat. They set out in the storm. The pelting rain had been so heavy, it had already eroded deep gullies in the road to the ranch. Rob cranked the windshield wipers up to maximum speed, but visibility was next to zero. As they headed uphill, the tires began to slip and slide in a gumbo of axle-deep mud.

Snuggled in Nell's arms, Katy was shivering so hard her teeth were rattling. Rob shifted into four-wheel drive. Still the wheels spun uselessly and the truck began to drift sideways. Mud sprayed up on the truck until it was coated from bottom to top.

They weren't getting anywhere. "It'll be worse getting stuck somewhere than not going at all," declared Nell.

Rob jammed the gears in a fury and screamed in frustration. "Why am I living in the middle of nowhere!"

"Rob . . ." Nell hushed him.

There was nothing else to do—they turned back. Nell held her jacket over Katy until they were in out of the rain, and Rob carried her up to her room again. Nell got on the phone to the medical clinic. Rob and Howard stood next to her, hanging on every word.

"I don't know if it's accurate. It's an old thermometer," she said, trying to keep her voice level, hiding the panic in her heart.

She covered the phone with her hand and looked at Rob. "They say they can't land a medevac in the storm."

She uncovered the phone. "Okay, we'll wait," she told the medic. "What do I look for?"

Her eyes closed as she listened to the answer.

"What kind of convulsions??" she cried.

Rob put his arms around her. Howard sat on the stairs and stared into space. Jack and Gus hung around on the porch in their slickers not knowing what to do.

Rob left Katy's room and went down the stairs. On the way down he glanced at the painting of the wild mustangs. Something about it arrested him in mid-step. He considered the image for a long time, as if he'd never really seen it before.

"Howard," he said, "stay by your mother. Don't leave her side."

"Dad, I . . ." Howard tried to find the words to express himself.

"Don't," said Rob.

"I'm sorry," he sobbed. "I really screwed up."

"No," declared Rob. He set his hand on his son's shoulder. "You're a good man."

Rob called out to Gus and Jack. "How bad is the horse?"

The men just stood there silently, not knowing what to say.

Rob looked at Jack knowingly. "Go back. Put her down."

Jack turned to leave, but his heart was full of doubt. He turned back to Rob. "She'll hear the shot."

"She'll think it's thunder," said Rob.

Jack stood, frozen. "No, she won't," he cried. "Katy is smart. She sees things, little details most people ignore . . . the ones that make a difference."

"She'll know it's Flicka," agreed Gus.

Rob thought about it. "But I can't let that animal suffer. I'll do it myself."

CHAPTER EIGHTEEN

Howard dumped a bucket of ice into the kitchen sink, and Nell refilled the ice pack for Katy. They brought it up to her bedroom. But to their surprise, Katy wasn't in bed!

She was standing in the living room in a kind of limp and ghostly delirium. She stared, hollow-eyed at her father who had just emerged from the office with his Winchester rifle.

"Are you going to kill Flicka?" she asked.

The sight of Katy overwhelmed him. "I'm just going to take a look at her," he said softly.

Howard and Nell dashed back downstairs. "Katy, what are you doing here?" asked Nell.

She automatically put her hand on Katy's forehead. The severity of the fever terrified her.

"It's okay, daddy. . . . You can shoot us," murmured Katy.

Nell burst into tears. "Come back to bed."

As she and Howard led Katy back upstairs, Rob burst out the door to the porch and let out a heartrending, gut-wrenching sob. How in the world had *everything* gone so wrong?

He pulled on his slicker, and rode back out into the storm. Lightning illuminated the landscape in eerie bursts. He rode along the high bank of Goose Creek. Before he saw Flicka, he heard her whimpering. He dismounted and went to her side.

Flicka lifted her head and looked at him. He raised his Winchester and took aim. But tears were clouding his sight. He wiped his eyes on the back of his sleeve and aimed again.

Flicka struggled to stand up. She managed to get one foot under her, then another. But she was too weak. She fell back to the ground and laid her head down in exhaustion.

Rob couldn't pretend he didn't see it. The filly still had

some fight left in her. He lowered his gun. "It's up to you now, girl."

Flicka whinnied sharply. She rolled her whole torso for momentum and again struggled to get on her feet.

Rob's horse seemed to answer her cry. The gelding reared up and pawed the air in terror. Rob realized that something more than his presence was upsetting Flicka. The gelding bolted for home.

Rob scanned the branches of the cottonwood trees overhead. There it was! A flash of tan fur moving behind the leaves! He heard the menacing, low growl, and he stepped back slowly, keeping his eyes trained on the cat.

Flicka cried out again and rocked her body, desperately trying to get up. The mountain lion lunged at her.

Rob took aim and fired.

The shot echoed across the valley.

Katy's feverish body shuddered at the sound. "*Flicka . . .*"

Without even thinking about it, Nell threw on her raincoat

and rushed outside. Gus and Jack were already sprinting out of the barn.

"I heard a shot," she told them.

"It was the Winchester," said Jack.

Howard came out to meet them. "Katy must've heard it, too."

Suddenly they heard a second shot ring out.

They looked at each other, confused.

"He wouldn't need a second shot," declared Jack.

Nell could hear the worry in Jack's voice. "Something's wrong," she cried.

The rain and thunder had tapered off. Nell ran to her horse and rode off into the fog toward Goose Creek. But before she arrived on the high bank, she spotted two figures moving slowly and cautiously in her direction. It was Rob, leading Flicka toward home. She rode up quietly alongside them, dismounted, and took Rob in her arms. She looked at Flicka.

"No good reason she's alive," said Rob.

"There's a very good reason." Nell ran her hand gently along the filly's neck. "She's got mustang blood in her. She's a fighter. Like our girl."

When they reached home, Jack and Gus ran out to greet them. They tucked Flicka safely in a warm, dry stable. And Nell and Rob returned to Katy's side. Rob dabbed her face with a cool, damp cloth. The sight of his daughter lying there so helpless dissolved the steely inner strength that had carried him through so many other crises.

He leaned over her bed and studied her face lovingly. "The day you were born and they gave you to me . . . I thought my hands were too rough to hold you," he whispered. "You cried every night, no matter what we did, but your mom said that was a good sign."

Nell leaned in the doorway and listened.

"You were strong. That wasn't much comfort when I was pacing with you back and forth all night. All you did was stare back at me with those big, beautiful eyes. So I made all kinds of promises to you, if you'd just go to sleep."

Rob sighed, longing only to see the sparkle in those eyes again. "Katy, I forgot to keep my promises. And I'm sorry. But if you'll stay with me . . ."

He broke down and sobbed. "I promise to tell you . . . every day . . . I'm so proud you're my daughter. Just . . . stay here. Please, Katy."

That night Nell slept next to Katy. Rob tucked the covers around them gently and gave them each a kiss. It was already after midnight. The storm had passed, and it seemed the whole world had gone silent. He glanced over at Katy's desk and happened to see her exam booklet lying open. He picked it up and flipped through it. Page after page was filled with Katy's writing. He pulled the chair up next to Katy's bed and began to read. When he'd finished, he quietly went to the computer and turned it on. He began to type, two fingers pecking slowly, one letter after the other.

CHAPTER NINETEEN

WHEN Nell woke up early the next morning, she was surprised to see Rob, head down, asleep at Katy's desk. Nell leaned over and squinted at the computer screen. She scrolled down the page and wept as she read Katy's words.

She addressed an e-mail to the headmaster of the Laramie Academy. She filled in the subject line: "Katherine McLaughlin, Final Essay," and clicked Send.

Gray and cloudy days passed, but when the bright July sun finally returned, its warming rays filtered through Katy's curtains, and she opened her eyes and looked around. She saw her father standing at the window, his head bowed.

"What's wrong, Daddy?" she asked.

Rob rushed to her side and felt her forehead. "Your fever's down," he cried.

She shut her eyes tight and tears trickled out. Her lips began to tremble, and she cried out in grief. "It's my fault Flicka's dead."

Rob took her hand. "Oh, I don't think so."

She studied his face, trying to understand what he meant.

He wrapped her in her blanket and swept her up in his arms. He carried her out the door to the porch and gave a loud whistle.

Katy looked out in the direction of the barn. "Flicka," she gasped, as her mother appeared around the corner leading the filly.

Her natural liveliness slowly returning, Flicka nodded and stepped toward Katy. Rob carried Katy across the yard to meet her horse. Howard followed close behind.

Katy pressed her hand against Flicka's neck. The wounds were already beginning to heal.

"Your mom's taking good care of her. But when you're better, I expect you to take care of her yourself," said Rob.

Katy looked at him intently. "But you said . . . If I don't get back into school . . ."

"Yeah, that's what I said," agreed Rob. "And I meant it."

"Dad sent them your essay," said Howard.

Katy was confused. She looked from Howard to her mom and then her dad. What was her brother talking about?

"I told them I don't know much about writing," explained Rob. "But I sure know about the west."

He swung Katy up onto Flicka's back. "And so does my daughter. And it's right in her essay. Every ornery, opinionated, hot-blooded part of it."

"Well . . . what did they say?" Katy asked.

Nell folded her arms across her chest. "What does anyone say to your father?"

"*Yes, sir!*" she and Howard cried in unison.

Katy laughed and stroked Flicka's neck, and Rob led them slowly back to the barn.

* * *

Before the end of that summer, it became necessary to hang an important attachment to the sign marking the entrance to Goose Creek Ranch. Under the lines: THE MCLAUGHLINS' QUARTER HORSES, Nell and Gus added the words MUSTANG RESCUE. Katy, Rob, and Jack inspected their fine handiwork and gave it their thumbs-up.

It wasn't long after that Howard finished packing up his room and headed off to college in Boston. As Katy stood at the end of the driveway waving good-bye, her eyes brimming over with tears, she smiled for him, too, acknowledging the wild courage he had found within himself. Howard had the strength he needed to break free of their father's expectations and create his own destiny. She pictured the wild mustangs in her favorite painting coming to life again and tearing across the wide open prairie, their manes and tails flying like banners in the wind.

"I believe there is a force in this world that lives beneath the surface . . . something primitive and wild that awakens when you need an extra push just to survive. Like wildflowers that bloom after a fire turns the forest black," Katy wrote in her essay.

"Most people are afraid of that wild force and keep it buried deep inside themselves, but there will always be a few people who have the courage to love what is untamed inside us. One of those men is my father.

"There was once a time when Americans came west to discover their destiny. Today they seem to move around every which way, restless and unsettled. But I think they're still looking for the same thing—a place where they can be optimistic about the future; a place that helps them to be who they really want to be, where they can feel that this life makes sense; a place where they can feel what I feel riding Flicka. Because when we're riding . . . all I feel is free."